JUST PLAIN BOB

CHUCK'S
Fantasy

Hot Romance Hardcore Erotica

WARNING

This book contains sexually explicit scenes and adult language. It may be considered offensive to some readers. This book is for sale to adults ONLY.

*   *   *   *   *   *   *   *   *   *   *   *   *   *   *   *   *   *   *   *

Please store your files wisely where they cannot be accessed by underage readers.

Please feel free to send me an email. Just know that these emails are filtered by my publisher. Good news is always welcome.

Just Plain Bob - **justplainbob@awesomeauthors.org**

About the Publisher

4Fun Publishing, a member of **BLVNP Incorporated**, 340 S. Lemon #6200, Walnut CA 91789, info@blvnp.com / legal@blvnp.com

NOTE: Due to the highly emotional reaction of some people to works of erotic fiction, any email sent to the above address that contains foul language or religious references is automatically deleted by our anti-spam software and will not be seen. All other communications are welcome.

DISCLAIMER

Please don't be stupid and kill yourself. This book is a work of FICTION. Do not try any new sexual practice that you find in this book. It is fiction and not to be confused with reality. Neither the author nor the publisher or its associates assume any responsibility for any loss, injury, death or legal consequences resulting from acting on the contents in this book. Every character in this book is over 18 years of age. The author's opinions are not to be construed as the opinions of the publisher. The material in this book is for entertainment purposes ONLY. Enjoy.

Is that why you showered last night?

Chuck and Lorrie were high school sweethearts who ended up together and got married. For ten years, they have kept their marriage healthy and taken turns in making each other happy.

One night, Chuck comes home late. Lorrie is waiting and eager to make love to him. She notices something strange – Chuck goes straight to the shower right after he gets inside the house. She finds it suspicious and figures out a way for Chuck to spill the beans.

Chuck's confession takes their marriage and sex life to a whole new level – one that is rip-roaring, at the same time, a walk on thin ice for their marriage.

Chuck's Fantasy

Hot Romance Erotica

By: Just Plain Bob

© **Just Plain Bob 2014**
ISBN: 978-1-68030-036-9

Chapter 1

I love my husband, I really do, and I'd bet money that he loves me, but that won't stop the divorce I see coming. When it comes time to apportion blame it will be a fifty-fifty split even though I could have stopped it at any time. But just as love is love, dumb is dumb and I was dumb enough to believe that Chuck knew what he wanted and that he could handle it when he got it.

~~***~~

Chuck and I had been high school sweethearts and then had maintained that relationship through college. After graduation we started out on our careers, mine in advertising and his in business. Six months after graduation we were married. Neither one of us wanted children so I went on the pill and for the next ten years, Chuck and I concentrated on our careers and on keeping each other happy. Things were fine until one night Chuck came home from playing poker at his boss' house.

I had been horny as horny as a goat all day and I was waiting up for Chuck when he got home and with every intention of getting myself laid. When he got home he was surprised to see me still awake and he became nervous when he found out why. Nervous and trying very hard to hide it. After ten years of marriage, four years of college and three years of high school with the man, I could tell when he was trying to keep something from me. Add to that the fact that he did something that he had never done before – taking a shower when coming home late – and I knew that he had been up to something. At the time I pushed it to the back of my mind because what was most important at that particular moment was getting my itch scratched. When Chuck came out of the bathroom I grabbed him and proceeded to wear him out.

The next morning the 'horny' was gone and in the cold, clear light of a new day I had questions, questions that Chuck did not want to furnish answers for. I am a persistent wench and I reminded Chuck of that fact and I let him know that I was going to stay after him like a dog worrying at a bone until I was satisfied. He finally bowed to the inevitable and told me about his poker night at the home of his boss.

~~***~~

Chuck had just been promoted to manager and it was his first time to be invited to the monthly poker game at Randy's house. For the first three hours, it had been seven men playing five and seven card stud and five card draw. Alice, Randy's wife, acted as hostess and served drinks and snacks. At the end of three hours of play Randy had announced that it was time for the last hand. He hollered out to Alice and when she came into the room he told her it was time for the last hand.

"Oh goody," she had said, "I'm more than ready," and then she had lifted her skirt, stepped out of her thong and had tossed it into the middle of the table. "Good luck guys," she said and then she left the room.

Now Chuck was a pretty damned good poker player – he had helped pay his way through college with winnings from fraternity house poker games – but he was also pretty good at office politics. Being the new guy he knew that it would be best if he not be a big winner the first few times he played so he had been getting and throwing in winning hands most of the night. Randy was dealing and he called the game – five-card draw, jacks or better to open and no limit on raises – and then he dealt the cards. Chuck checked his cards and saw that he had three jacks. He figured that he could get away with taking the last pot without upsetting anyone, but it soon became apparent that something that he didn't understand was going on. The betting started to get stupid and he could tell that the others were trying to force each other out of the hand and he decided to bail out. He tossed in his three jacks and sat back to watch.

The players drew cards and then there was a lot more betting and finally the cards were laid down and Phil took the hand with two pair. He reached for the pot, but took only the thong and left the money and got up and headed for the living room. Everybody got up and followed him. In the living room, there was a chair sitting in the middle of the room and Phil went straight to it and sat down. A minute or so later, music started playing and Alice danced into the room and did a slow and sensuous strip. Once down to nothing but 'Come Fuck Me' pumps, she went over to Phil and pulled his trousers and boxers off and then gave him a full contact lap dance. When the music stopped, she knelt in front of Phil and started sucking his cock.

Chuck looked around for Randy and saw him standing off to the side videotaping the action. Phil told Alice that he was going to cum and she took her mouth off of him and held it a couple of inches away and jacked him off with her hand. When he came, the cum shot up like a fountain into Alice's mouth and then she lowered her head and finished the blowjob by sucking him dry. Then Alice stood up and licked her lips as she looked around the room at the other men and then she said, "Okay guys, let's take it to the bedroom."

She headed for the bedroom and all the men followed along behind her and Chuck followed along to see what would happen next. What happened next was a gangbang. Alice got on the bed, spread her legs and said, "Who wants to be first?" and then she took on everybody there while Randy taped the affair.

"Everybody there? Are you telling me that you took part?"

Chuck looked away from me and I said, "Don't you look away from me Chuck. Did you screw that woman? Is that why you showered last night? To wash the smell of her off you?"

Still looking away he mumbled a 'yes' and then he turned to face me and rushed into an explanation. "It didn't mean anything honey, honest to God it didn't. She was lying on the bed looking at me and telling me I was next and when I hesitated she said, 'What's the matter sweetie, you too good for Alice?' I saw Randy looking at me and I didn't know what he would do if I turned his wife down and so I did it with her."

"I know you, Chuck and I know that there is a little more to it than that." He got a sheepish look on his face and I said, "Spit it out Chuck, you know I won't quit until I get it all."

He took a deep breath, "It was the most mind blowing thing I had ever seen in my life. One after another they fucked her and she just kept calling out next when one man would finish. She begged them to make her cum, to get hard for her, to fuck her harder and faster and when the other guys were done they were all looking at me and all I could think of was what she would feel like after those other five guys. I wanted to do it. I wanted to stick my cock in her to feel what the mess left by the other five would feel like. I wanted to, but still I hesitated because I can't hide anything from you and I knew that you wouldn't like it, not one bit. But then she did the 'You too good for me' bit and I saw Randy watching me to see what I would do and so I did it. And then it got weird. She wanted two men at once and then three. Once she had all six of us."

"All six? How could she do that?"

"She was sitting on Phil with his cock in her pussy while George was pushing his cock in her ass. Mike and Roger were standing in front of her and she was alternating between them as she sucked their dicks. Bill and I stood next to her so she could jack us off with her hands while Phil held her steady in an upright position."

"How many times?"

"How many times what?"

"How many times did you fuck the bitch?"

He looked away from me again and mumbled something.

"I didn't hear that Chuck."

"Four, I did it four times with her. Twice in her pussy and once each in her mouth and ass, but honest to God honey, it didn't mean anything."

"Just being one of the guys, huh?"

"Yeah, that's all it was, just trying to fit in."

"And all Randy did was furnish the slut and take pictures?"

"Yeah, that was all he did. I guess his turn on is watching Alice."

~~***~~

Things were a little cool around our house for a while after that, but we did manage to work through it. It helped that I loved Chuck and that there was no doubt in my mind that he loved me. I did make it crystal clear to him that there would be no more poker games at Randy's. He agreed, but the damage was already done although it wouldn't surface for another couple of months or so. To sum it up, Chuck got so turned on by the idea of Randy watching Alice that he started wondering what it would be like to watch me. He never mentioned it to me, just kept it to himself as a fantasy, but that fantasy changed him.

It wasn't noticeable right away; just little things that I didn't pick up on at first like the way he looked at me after we made love. He had always given me clothes as part of my gifts on birthdays, anniversaries and at Christmas, but suddenly they got more revealing, sexier and he started telling me what he would like to see me wear when we went out. While he had always bought me clothes he had never bought me shoes. It was the shoes that finally woke me up to what was going on. Chuck started giving me strappy sandals, pumps, slingbacks and all had four or five inch heels.

Suddenly, it dawned on me that Chuck was seeing to it that I dressed to attract male attention. After I figured that out, I ran a test to see if I was right. Chuck took me to a dance at the Elks one Saturday night and I put on the most revealing dress I own. A little black number that was backless and cut so low in the front that to wear a bra would have ruined the line of the dress so I wore it without a bra and as a result a lot of my breasts were on display. With the dress I wore thigh highs and a pair of CFMs with five inch heels. Chuck's hard on was so evident when he saw how I was dressed that I wasn't sure he would let me out of the house.

At the dance, I watched Chuck and saw that Chuck was watching the men who were looking at me. It was obvious that Chuck wanted other men to look at me, but why? Was it an "Eat your heart out, she belongs to me" kind of thing? Or was he just proud of me. Call me naïve, but it was another three months before I figured it out and only then by accident.

Chuck was out of town on a business trip and I decide one night to replace the window blinds in the family room. Chuck doesn't like leaving his car at the airport when he is on trips so I usually drive him to the airport or he cabs downtown and takes the light rail out to the airport. As a result, I have his car at home when he is on a trip and since the trunk of his car is a lot bigger than the trunk of my little two seat Miata convertible I drove his car to Target. I bought what I needed and when I went to load it into the trunk, I had to move a heavy box out of the way to get things to fit.

Once home, I unloaded the trunk and then got curious about the heavy box and so I opened it and what I found was about six months worth of men's magazines. Gallery, Penthouse, Penthouse Letters, Penthouse Forum and Variations just to name a few. You know how sometimes when you pick up a book it will fall open to the page you were on when you put it down? The first magazine I picked up did just that. I fell open to a section called "Someone's Watching" and I read some of it. It was all about men who liked watching their wives with other men. I check the rest of the magazines and saw that they all had sections on men watching other men fuck their wives. I further noticed that the pages that were dog-eared were all in sections where the wife got it on with some one other than her husband.

That's when the penny dropped. I remembered Chuck's fascination with the way Randy watched Alice, the way he was dressing me to grab other men's attention, and now this – books on wife watching. Chuck wanted to watch me!

Chapter 2

I carried the box of magazines into the house, poured myself a glass of wine and settled down to read. I read and sipped wine from five in the afternoon until eleven-thirty and when I climbed into bed I was so hot and horny that I did something that I hadn't done in ten years – I masturbated! I was so horny from reading those stories that my pussy was on fire. I'm not just talking about the wife watching stories either. The girl on girl, black on white, swinging and swapping, straying and wayward wives also got to me. The only ones that left me cold were the boy on boy ones.

The next day, I took a couple of the magazines to work with me and read them during coffee breaks and lunch hour. That afternoon, one of the girls I work with told me that some of the others from the office were going to be stopping after work for drinks and asked me if I would like to join them. Chuck was not going to be home for two more days and I had nothing to hurry home for so I said I would. The waitress wasn't even back with our drink order before men were coming over to us and asking us to dance. Being the only married woman at the table, I didn't think it would be wise so I said no thanks and I just sat, sipped my drink and watched.

While I watched I began to have strange thoughts. I'd look at a guy and wonder what he might be like in bed. Another guy had me wondering if he ate pussy and if so, was he any good at it. My head was full of stories from the magazines and as I looked around the room at the men there I was matching them up with a story. The table where two men were busy talking; would one of them like to fuck me while I sucked on the other? Would those six guys over shooting pool at the pool tables like to gangbang me? I saw the bartender looking at me and I wondered if he would like me to be on my knees behind the bar sucking his cock while he waited on customers. Those two black men sitting off to the side of the dance floor, did they have huge black cocks? Was it true that if you go black you never go back?

I was squirming on the seat as I drove home that night. I rushed into the house and masturbated and then I sat down and read magazines for three hours and masturbated one more time before going to bed.

~~***~~

The next day during my lunch hour, I visited an adult bookstore and bought myself a rubber dildo and a battery-operated vibrator. While there, I got curious and went into the arcade section, went into one of the booths and fed a couple of dollar bills into the machine. I'd never seen porn videos before and I sat there fascinated as I watched all kinds of sex flashing across the screen in front of me. I stopped hitting the selector button when the videos got to one where three men were fucking one girl. She had one in her rectum, one in her vagina and one in her mouth and I remembered how Chuck had described Alice doing that.

I sat there and watched and wondered what it would be like to be that girl and I slid my skirt up, ran my hand inside my panty and masturbated. While fingering myself I saw some movement out of the corner of my eye and for the first time I noticed that there was a hole in the wall between my booth and the one nest to it. In the flickering light from the screen, I thought I saw eyes watching me.

I have no idea what possessed me to do what I did next. I stood up, removed my panties and then sat back down with my skirt up around my waist and my legs spread wide so the voyeur could get a good look and then I started to finger fuck myself. Just as I felt the orgasm rushing through me, a large black cock came through the hole in the wall. I stared at it in fascination. I'd read about glory holes in the magazines and here I was, Mrs. Middle-aged Housewife, sitting in a booth in an adult bookstore and looking at the first hard cock other than my husband's that I had seen since getting married.

I bent forward to look at it close. I could see one of the veins that ran along the top throbbing and the cock itself was twitching – making little up and down bounces – and for kicks, I lowered my mouth to within inches of it and then blew on it with my hot breath. There was a drop of pre-cum in the pee hole and I was tempted to stick out my tongue and lick it up. Did I dare? No, no I didn't, but I did reach out and wrap my fingers around it just to feel the heat of it. As soon as my hand closed around it, the owner of it started to hump my hand and I wondered if I stayed there and held it would it spurt for me?

I checked my watch and saw that I still had twenty minutes of my lunch period left and it was a five minute walk back to work so I stayed where I was and held onto the black cock while it fucked my hand. As the time ticked down, I became obsessed with getting it off before I left and I started stroking it instead of just gripping it. I was getting desperate to make it cum and I was only seconds away from taking it in my mouth when it finally erupted. It shot spurt after spurt into my booth and I let go of it and leaned back against the wall. I was astonished at what I had just done. That wasn't me. That wasn't the sort of person I was. What in God's name had gotten into me?

I used my panty to wipe the goop off my hand and then went to put it in my purse. It dawned on me that it was soaking wet and if I put it in my purse I would get the strangers cum all over everything else in there so I dropped it on the floor and pushed it into a corner with my toe. I straightened my skirt and left the booth and I noticed the door to the next booth was open and no one was in it. There were six men, three of them black, on the store side of the wall and I glanced at them as I headed for the door and wondered which one of the black men it had been. I left the store knowing that I would never know.

~~***~~

That evening as I rushed home, I felt so wicked at what I had done that my pussy was dripping. That night I used my dildo and my vibrator to get myself off – several times – as I sat on the couch, sipped wine and read more magazines.

The next day was the last day of Chuck's trip and he would be gone one more night so when Sheila asked me if I wanted to stop with her and some of the other girls for a drink after work I said yes. It was the same as it had been the night before; we had no sooner sat down than men were asking us to dance. This time I said yes and got up and danced like the other girls.

Over the course of the next two hours, I had hands on my ass and breasts, and a dozen hard cocks pushed into my leg. One guy even started to run his hand down the inside the front of my skirt and I was so hot and horny that I almost – only almost – let him reach his goal. I had several invitations to make a trip out to the parking lot or to a motel and two guys asked me if they could go home with me.

I wondered if I could do it, if I could take some guy home with me and fuck his eyes out while Chuck watched. It was then that I suddenly realized that I wanted to do it. I wanted to fuck some stranger while my husband watched. All of a sudden, Chuck and I had matching fantasies, or maybe we did. I was just guessing that his fantasy was watching me with other men. I had to admit that I really didn't know just which letters turned him on. I just hoped to God it wasn't the boy/boy ones.

~~***~~

Chuck wasn't home two minutes before I had his pants down around his ankles and I was on my knees with his cock in my mouth. It was one in the morning when I finally gave up trying to get him up again. After he fell asleep, I went into the bathroom where I used my dildo to give myself two more orgasms before finally going to bed. I lay there looking up at the ceiling and wondered how to make my fantasy (and Chuck's) come true. I wanted to do it, but I wasn't going to fuck another man behind my husband's back. The question was, did Chuck really want to see me with another man, or was it just a fantasy that he never actually wanted to happen? If he really didn't want it then my broaching the subject could do great harm to our marriage. No, I couldn't make the first move – Chuck had to do that.

There were other questions too. Could I actually fuck another man with Chuck watching? That I could fuck another man was a foregone conclusion. It had taken every last little bit of my will power to keep me from accepting one of those parking lot invitations that night at the bar. Next question was even if Chuck really wanted it, could he handle it? There was sometimes a very big difference between wanting and actually getting. What was the old saying, "Be careful what you wish for, you just might get it?" I wanted to do it; I wanted to do it in the worst way, but I loved Chuck and I didn't want to screw up my marriage. I tossed and turned for hours before I finally fell asleep.

~~***~~

A week went by; a week during which all I thought about was having my fantasy actually happen. On Wednesday, the thoughts had me so horny that I felt myself drawn back to the adult bookstore and my visit was a carbon copy of my first visit. I masturbated while unknown eyes watched me through the glory hole and when a cock came through the hole I took it in my hand and stroked it while I fingered myself. It was a surprise when I had an orgasm just as the hard white cock in my hand shot thick ropy streams of cum onto the floor of my booth. Once again I used my panties to clean my hands and then I tossed them into a corner and hurried back to work.

Once back at work, I sat at my desk and stared out the window and thought about what I wanted. I came to realize that Chuck might never mention his fantasies to me and I needed him to. I wanted to do it, but it had to be Chuck's idea. In order for my marriage to go on, to keep me from cheating on Chuck, my fucking another man had to be his idea. In a rare moment of pure truth I realized that I didn't care if Chuck got to watch or not as long as I got to ride another man's cock, but it absolutely had to be Chuck's idea. The problem was how to make him have that idea.

I racked my brain for weeks to come up with a way to nudge Chuck into bringing his fantasies out in the open. I felt that if I could get him to talk about it I could gently steer things to the point where he would ask me if I had any interest. The idea I finally came up with was simplicity itself and I couldn't understand why it wasn't the first thing I thought of. After finding Chuck's stash of magazines and getting turned on reading them, I took to buying Penthouse Letters and reading it at work. I was sitting in my office tearing open the cellophane wrapper on the latest issue when the little subscription card fell out of the package and onto my desk. I looked at it and the light bulb went on over my head. Chuck's birthday was in two weeks. I filled out the card, made a copy of it and mailed it in. On Chuck's birthday he opened his birthday card and found the copy of the subscription card.

"What's this?"

"One of your birthday presents, a two year subscription to Penthouse Letters."

"Why would you give me something like that?"

"I used your car on your last business trip and I found the box of magazines in the trunk. I thought that if you liked that kind of thing you might like to have a subscription. Besides, I read some of them and some of the things in them turned me on. I figured that if I got you a subscription I could read it when you finish it."

I saw something change in his eyes when I said that and then he did just what I had hoped he would do.

"What turned you on?"

"Lots of things, but mostly, it was the overall sexual content."

"Oh come on baby, there must have been something in particular. What was it?"

"You won't laugh at me or get mad?"

"No, of course not."

"The ones on oral sex."

"Why would that be a turn on? We have oral sex all the time."

"Not that way."

"What way?"

"When I have cum in me. The thought of you sucking cum out of my pussy gets me all hot and horny."

"You want to fuck another man and then have me go down on you?"

"No silly, I want you to lick my pussy after you make love to me."

I saw the light start to die in his eyes so I quickly said, "The other thing that turned me on was the section called Some Ones Watching. I don't know why but spying on some one while they are making love sounds as erotic as all get out."

"How about being the one spied on?"

"What do you mean?"

"Could you make love if some one was watching you?"

"Good Lord Chuck, how did we get on this subject? All I did was give you a subscription to a magazine. Come on, let's open the rest of your presents."

The idea was planted and now all I had to do was wait.

~~***~~

It didn't take long. Chuck's birthday was Wednesday and on Saturday, as we were dressing to go to a party, Chuck said, "Do you have any fantasies honey?"

"Sure. My favorite is where I win the lottery, buy an island in the South Seas and spend the rest of my life on the beach perfecting my tan."

"No, no honey, I mean sexual fantasies."

"Just the one I already mentioned."

"What was that?"

"Honestly, don't men ever pay any attention to anything a woman says?"

"What did I miss?"

"On your birthday I told you that the thought of you eating your cum out of my pussy made me hot and horny."

"I don't think I could lick my stuff out of you."

"How about some one else's then?"

"What! What did you just say?"

I laughed, "Don't have a cow sweetie, I was just joking. You should see the look on your face right now – it's priceless."

I was rolling my nylons on while Chuck watched and I saw the lump in his pants start to grow:

"How about you? Do you have any sexual fantasies?"

"A couple."

"You want to tell me about them?"

"No."

"Why not?"

"Because I don't think that you would like hearing about them."

"Oh come on Chuck, they can't be any worse than the letters that turn you on when you're reading your magazines."

Chuck was silent and I said, "What's the matter baby, are they about me?"

He turned away from me and I said, "That's it, isn't it? You are having fantasies about me. What are they? Me with another girl? Me with a big black nigger who has a fifteen-inch cock and who uses me as his personal fuck toy? Come on baby, tell me, it just might turn me on."

"You promise that you won't get mad?"

"Of course I won't get mad. You are just going to tell me a fantasy not ask or make me do anything. Come on, tell me. Do you imagine me getting gangbanged? Come on baby, spill it. You know I'm just going to hack away at you until you do."

"Okay, but if you laugh or get mad at me I'm going to be severely pissed. My fantasy is to watch you make love to other men."

"Other men, not man?"

"It started out as another man and evolved into other men."

"Oh wow. I never considered that."

"Does that mean you have considered other things?"

"Well yeah, but nothing like that."

"What did you consider doing?"

"Like doing some of that role playing. You know, go into a bar and flirt, lead men on, get felt up and then hurry home and screw our brains out. But me and other guys while you watch? Wow babe, I don't think I could do that. I don't know if I could do it with one man, let alone several."

"You say you don't think you could, does that leave the door open to maybe finding out?"

Things were heading where I wanted them to go so I decided not to push my luck and try to rush things. "I don't know Chuck. It is one thing to fantasize about things, but something else again to actually try them. Besides, I took a vow at our wedding to be faithful to you."

"You aren't being unfaithful if you do it with my approval."

"How did we get onto this subject anyway? Go take your shower or we will be late for the party."

~~***~~

At the party I made sure that I punched all of Chuck's buttons. I was wearing one of the outfits that he had given me and CFMs with five-inch heels. I danced with anyone who asked and I allowed hands to go where ever they wanted. My ass was squeezed, my pussy was rubbed through my skirt and I just knew I was going to have bruises on my breasts when I got home. I let myself get maneuvered into dark corners, let myself be kissed and even gave some tongue to a couple of guys.

I did all of that with one eye on Chuck to see how he was taking it. He wasn't smiling, but I didn't see anger either so I took it to the next level. When my next dance partner, a tall, handsome black man named Mark, suggested we step outside for some air I said okay and three minutes later we were swapping tongues. He worked his hand down the inside of my skirt and panties and I rubbed the bulge in his pants with my hand. When his hand reached my pussy I unzipped him and reached inside, grasped his erection and pulled it out to where I could stroke it. I looked down at it and saw that it wasn't all that big, just a bit fatter than Chuck's, but no longer.

"Let's go to my car," Mark whispered.

"No, I can't," I said as I let go of his cock and started pulling away from him. "I can't do this. I'm a married woman and I've never cheated on my husband before."

"Maybe not, but you want to or we wouldn't be here doing what we are."

"But I can't. He's inside and he may come looking for me any minute now," and I pulled away from him and hurried back into the party.

~~***~~

We were no sooner in the car to go home when Chuck said, "Got a little carried away tonight did you?" I was thinking on how to answer that when he said, "I saw you and Mark out on the patio. Several other people saw it to."

"Your point?"

"Damn it Loretta, don't you think that shows everyone how low you regard me when you can act like that in front of me?"

"It bothered you?"

"Yes it did."

"Did it anger you, make you want to kick Mark's ass?"

"Damned right, it did."

"Well, that is just what I was trying to find out. Remember our little talk, the one we had in the bedroom?"

"Yes, what about it?"

"I thought about it all the way to the party. The more I thought about it the more I wondered about what it would be like and the more I wondered about what it would be like the more I thought about maybe doing it. I almost had myself talked into trying it and then reality set in."

"What do you mean, reality?"

"I'm not stupid Chuck. I've seen you change over this last year and I know what changed you. Randy's poker party and what his slut did changed you. The same man who became incensed if a man danced too close with me was suddenly buying me sexy outfits and pressing me to wear them in public, to attract attention from the same men who pissed you off when they danced to close. Tonight you told me of your fantasy of seeing me make it with other men and the way you said it and the tone of your voice told me that it was more that just a fantasy – you actually wanted me to do it!

"I like doing things for you Chuck, I like doing what makes you happy and while being bedded by another man is stretching things a bit I wouldn't rule it out if that is what you really wanted. The other side of that coin is that I love you and I value my marriage and I'm not – repeat not – going to do anything that will jeopardize either of those. So tonight, I did what I did to see how you would react. Your reaction to what I did tonight tells me that there isn't any way on God's Green Earth that you could handle seeing me in bed with another man."

"You mean you really thought about doing it?"

"Until we got in this car, but not now, no way!"

"Why not?"

"Get serious Chuck, you couldn't handle seeing me felt up and being kissed. The fact that I stroked Mark's cock bent you all out of shape; there is no way you could handle seeing me fuck another man."

"The party was different Loretta. I wasn't in on it. If I had known what you were doing I'd have felt like I was part of it."

"That's what you say now, but I have no way of knowing whether or not it is just bullshit and I'm not risking my marriage on bullshit."

"Okay, I'll just have to prove it isn't."

"How do you figure you can do that?"

"Harry Winslow's wife is throwing him a birthday party next Saturday. I hadn't intended on going, but now I think we will. You just go and do whatever you feel comfortable with only this time I'll know and that will make me a part of it."

"Whatever I feel comfortable with doing?"

"No pressure Lorrie, just do what you want."

~~***~~

I was well on my way to doing what I wanted to do and with my husband's blessings. The only problem was that it was a week away and the anticipation was driving me crazy. By Wednesday, I was so frustrated that I was ready to scream so during my lunch break I headed for the adult bookstore.

This time a cock came through the hole in the wall before I even put my money into the machine. I stared at it for several seconds and then I went to my knees in front of it. The cock that was sticking through the wall was black and it was huge! It had to be twelve inches long because he had ten inches sticking out on my side of the wall. I was staring at the drop of pre-cum in the pee hole and something happened as I was reaching for it. I don't know why it happened; I hadn't planned on it happening, but at the last second my tongue slid out and I licked the head of that huge cock. A tenth of a second later I was giving some unknown man a blowjob. He must have been as excited about it as I was because it only took him about three minutes to get off. I wasn't expecting it and when the first glob hit the back of my throat, I jerked back and the second spurt hit my nose and the third hit my chin. I grabbed the cock with both hands and finished him off by hand.

As the limp cock pulled back and disappeared I got my panties off and wiped off my face and hands with them and then I tossed them into a corner. As I did I wondered what happened to all the panties I was leaving in that booth. I giggled at the thought that they might be pinned to a board somewhere all in a row and with a label under them; maybe something like "Booth C, 6/5/05." I still had my problem though so I fed some money into the machine and masturbated while watching a sexy little blond take on three black men. I got myself off, but Chuck was still going to be worn out when I got done with him that night.

~~***~~

Even though I knew I'd crossed a line with what I had done at the bookstore I didn't consider it as cheating on Chuck. As far as I was concerned, cheating was giving yourself to another man and I hadn't done that and I wasn't going to do that. If I gave myself to another it would only be with my husband's blessings. I wanted that blessing, oh sweet Jesus, did I ever want it. I had a list of guys I wanted to take to my bed, but I was stone serious about loving Chuck and not wanting to screw up my marriage. So, even though I wanted other men I wasn't going to do it without Chuck's approval and I wanted to make damned sure that we were on the same page.

An hour before it was time to get ready for Harry's party I told Chuck that I wanted to talk to him. "About tonight, are you absolutely sure about what you want? Have you thought about it all the way through?"

"What do you mean?"

"Outside of the fact that I'm no so sure that you can handle me being with another man, have you given any thought to the rest of it? What if you decide that you don't really like it, but that I do and I want to do more of it? Have you considered that he might be big, a lot bigger than you and I'll get hooked on having big cocks? What about the possibility that he might be a better lover and I'll want to continue seeing him? Have you considered any of those things?"

"Not really. They don't really matter to me."

"How can you say that?"

"Look Loretta, I love you and I know that you love me. All of those things that you just mentioned could happen and it wouldn't matter because I know that you will always come home to me. I know that I might be letting the genie out of the bottle and you might run free for a while, but I also know that you are mine and that I am yours and I have no doubt that whatever happens that won't change."

~~***~~

The party was an hour old when Mark showed up. I felt my pussy tingle as I remembered what we had done at the last party. As I thought about the black cocks from the adult bookstore and about Mark's nice sized black boner I turned to Chuck and whispered in his ear, "Are you absolute certain you can handle me with another man?"

"Yes."

I looked at him for several seconds and then I said, "Okay, but before I bring a man into our bedroom I want to make sure. I'm going to run a little test. When you see me dancing with Mark go outside and find a place where you can watch our car without being seen."

"What are you going to do?"

"At the very least I'll give him a hand job. If you don't come storming over to rip the doors off the car I may go down on him. Where it might go from there I don't know, but I'd rather find out here than at home that you can't handle it."

"You are serious? You are really going to do it?"

"I guess that depends on you, doesn't it?"

~~***~~

It didn't take Mark long to come over and ask me to dance and it didn't take long for his hands to go roaming. When he leaned down and whispered in my ear, "Any chance we can go outside and pick up where we left off last week?" I glanced around and saw Chuck heading outside.

"Am I any less married tonight than I was last week?"

"No, but you have had a week to think about it. You want to sweetie and we both know it. The fact that you were the one to unzip me and take my cock out proved that."

"Did Chuck do something to you and you feel the need to get even by having his wife?"

"No sweetie, I want you because you are the sexiest woman I've ever seen."

He had me in a dark corner and he had a hand on my right breast and I was rubbing his hard cock with my leg. I slid a hand down his body until I reached his bulge and then I squeezed it. "Do you have a condom?"

"As a matter of fact I do."

"Why don't we go outside for a breath of fresh air?"

"Lead the way, fair lady."

I led him straight to our car and on the way I tried to see if I could spot Chuck, but I never saw him. Mark and I got in the back and started to make out like teenagers at the drive in. Mark's hands were busy on my breasts and I was tugging at his zipper while our tongues played with each other. I lifted my skirt so Mark could get my panties down while I tried to work his cock out of confinement. His fingers found my pussy just as his cock sprang free and I spread my legs to give him better access as I started to jack him off. Our tongues were still dueling and I was moaning and squirming as Mark fingered me.

As much as I wanted to let myself go, there was still a part of me that expected Chuck to come charging up to put a stop to things. When, after almost five minutes he still hadn't tried to stop me I took it to the next level. I pulled my mouth away from Mark's and lowered my head and took his nice hard black cock between my lips and started sucking on it. I licked it, I sucked it and I used my hands to play with his balls. It wasn't long, less than three minutes actually, before I felt him tense up and I knew he was going to release his load and I clamped my lips tight around him as he gushed. I gulped and I swallowed and when he stopped spurting and started to go soft I kept on making love to his cock with my mouth.

It took a few minutes, but then I felt him starting to grow and I took my mouth off him and asked him for his condom. He gave it to me and I rolled it on and then I slid down on the seat and told him to fuck me. Mark was only marginally bigger than Chuck and since I'd been a virgin when I married Chuck I had no yardstick for measuring a man's ability as a lover, but the fact that I was a married woman and that somewhere close by my husband was watching me get fucked by another man was so exciting that I had an orgasm almost as soon as Mark plunged his cock into me.

I moaned, I screamed, I cried out and I pushed up at him to meet each of his down strokes and I came again and again before Mark climaxed. I felt so deliciously wicked and slutty as I lay stretched out on that back seat that I almost went after myself with my fingers so that I could cum again. Mark was leaning over me and he said, "That was marvelous. When can we do it again?"

I only hesitated a moment and then I asked, "Have you got another condom?"

"In my car."

"Better hurry then, I only have so much time before Chuck misses me and comes looking."

Chapter 3

The ride home was silent which wasn't a real surprise to me. Chuck had been quiet since returning to the party. I had no idea how he had taken what I'd done; his only response to my, "Well, was it what you wanted?" was "We will talk about it later." The rest of the party he busied himself talking with friends and he pretty much ignored me. I was beginning to think that I had the answer to the question of whether or not he could handle me being with another man and the answer was no. It looked like Mark was going to be my first and only extra-marital affair. Suddenly, I was glad he screwed me the second time.

Mark had just cum and I had been lying on that backseat in that dreamy state I get in after having an orgasm (or in that case – several) and Mark had asked when we could do it again. He was asking me what day we could meet again, but I had looked up at him and asked if he had another condom. He had pulled on his pants and run for his car to get one out of the glove compartment. I had expected Chuck to run up to the car as soon as Mark left, but he didn't.

When Mark got back with the fresh condom, I sucked his cock hard again and then I rolled the rubber on him. He went to mount me, but I stopped him and told him I wanted to be on top. He lay on his back and I lowered myself onto his black hardness and began to ride him. In less than a minute, I had another orgasm and it wasn't from just the fucking. As I had been sliding up and down on Mark's beautiful black cock I had been looking around for Chuck. When I found him, my eyes met his and at that moment I felt so slutty and wicked and the erotic excitement of fucking another man while looking into my husband's eyes triggered my orgasm and just as it hit, I blew Chuck a kiss. When I finished spasming I looked again, but Chuck was gone and I didn't see him again until I returned to the party.

After my initial orgasm (of the second round) Mark pulled me down, rolled me over on my back and began fucking me hard. I had two more orgasms before he finally came and as we were rearranging our clothes prior to going back into the party, Mark asked me when we could get together again. I wanted to say, "How about tomorrow?" but I couldn't because I had no idea how Chuck was going to act now that I had done what he wanted.

"I'm still a married woman Mark and I'm not looking for a boyfriend or a full time lover. What I wanted was an experience. I obviously enjoyed it, but I don't know how I'm going to feel about it when I wake up tomorrow. Give me a couple of days to think about it and then call me."

I sent him inside and I waited for almost ten more for Chuck to show up and when he didn't I went inside and got as fresh drink. A few minutes later I saw Chuck come in and I took that as a bad sign. He was out there, why hadn't he come over to the car when Mark went inside? I thought that and the "We will talk about it later," pretty much put an end to the fun I was planning on having.

~~***~~

We were almost home before I worked up enough courage to broach the subject. "Are you going to talk to me or do I just plan on packing when we get home?"

"Why would you pack?"

"Well obviously things did not go well tonight, at least from your perspective. You wouldn't talk to me at the party and you haven't said a word since we got in the car and I don't know why you are pissed at me. I asked you at least a dozen times if you really wanted me to do it and if you were sure you could handle it and every time you said yes."

"I am not pissed off at you."

"Then why aren't you talking to me?"

"Because I am pissed off, but not at you. I haven't been talking because I'm afraid I'll say the wrong thing and you might take it wrong. I've been waiting until I cool down before I open my mouth."

"I don't understand."

"What I wanted was to watch you with another man, not for you to fuck another man. The key word there is 'watch'. Knowing that another man was fucking you didn't do a thing for me. I needed to watch, to see it happen. I didn't see a fucking thing tonight! It didn't matter where I stood I couldn't see shit. I knew it was happening, but I couldn't get close enough to see without that asshole seeing me."

"Asshole? I thought you liked Mark."

"I did before he stabbed me in the back by fucking my wife. And while we are on the subject, why Mark? Why did you pick a nigger?"

"A nigger? Since when have you been a racist?"

"Since the asshole fucked you behind my back."

"Well for your information, I picked Mark because he was black. If I was going to do this for you I wanted it to be an experience for me too. I'd never had anything to do with black men before Mark and I wondered if there was a difference between black and white."

"Is there?"

"No, not really. His cock is a little fatter than yours, but yours is a little longer than his. But we do have a problem. If I am hearing you right you still want me to do another man while you watch, right?"

"Yes."

"Well, I never planned on doing it except with people I know and that I feel I can trust; both trust to be clean and trust to keep quiet about it and not blab it all over so every one starts thinking I'm the neighborhood slut. To me that means the men who travel in our social circle and that I know fairly well."

"Can't you do it with the guys you work with? Guys that I really don't know all that well and only see at company picnics and Christmas parties?"

"There isn't anyone of them I would feel comfortable with. I only know them at work; I don't know anything at all about their personal lives. I mean Danny seems like a nice enough guy at work, but what does he do when he leaves? Does he see prostitutes, pick up strange women in bars and could he have picked up a disease from one of them? At least with the men in our social circle I can feel somewhat safe."

"I don't know. I guess I'm going to have to think about it."

"Let me know. I know you must feel frustrated over tonight and Mark wanted to know if we could do it again and if so when. I told him to call me in a couple of days so when he calls I need to know whether to invite him over or tell him it was all a big mistake and that I can't ever let it happen again."

As we pulled into the driveway I reached over and rubbed Chuck's cock through his pants. "Did knowing that your wife was a whore tonight make you horny? Did knowing that she had a big black cock in her mouth make your dick twitch? That the same big black cock was in her pussy twice tonight and that she loved it?"

I felt his cock grow under my hand and I grinned. "I can't offer you real honest to God sloppy seconds because I made him wear a rubber both times, but he might have loosened me up enough that you will be able to tell that you aren't the first one to go in there tonight. Would you like that honey? Would you like my black lover's leftovers? Would you like to be the second man to fuck me in less than four hours?"

"Jesus Loretta, what the hell has gotten into you?"

"Well, so far Mark has and now I'm trying to get you into me. Don't be so shocked baby, you had to know that having me fuck other men would make me a slut and now that I am a slut don't be surprised when I act like one. You going to fuck me or not?'

Chuck damned near dragged me out of the car and into the house and he did actually rip my blouse off in his haste to strip me naked. I was pure slut for him that night and I did things with and to him that I had never done before. I sucked his cock while ass fucking him with my fingers; I licked his asshole and I let him fuck me in my ass and then I did the sluttiest thing I could think of – I sucked his cock right after he had pulled it out of my ass. His cock was in my mouth, my pussy, and my ass or in one of my hands for three solid hours. I fucked him into exhaustion and as he slept I got myself off one more time with my dildo. As I was fading off to sleep I was already planning my next extra-marital affair.

~~***~~

Sunday morning, I was up before Chuck and I was sitting at the kitchen table sipping coffee and working on a list of possible bed partners. Actually, I was working on two different lists. The A list was all the men who moved in our social circle and who I would like to try and just in case Chuck dug in his heels and said no to them I was also working on a B list. The B list was mostly guys I worked with although I did put down the name of that cute bartender at Adolph's.

I knew from the night before that Chuck was going to want me to do it at least once more. I figured that the best way to see that we didn't stop any time soon was to fuck Chuck's eyes out. I would give him five times the sex we usually had and when he commented on it I would tell him that giving him his fantasy was so sexually exciting that I was constantly horny.

In keeping with that plan, I did not leave him alone at all on Sunday. I followed him around and interrupted everything that he tried to do. I had him take me on the hood of the car in the garage when he was trying to reline the front brakes. He got an extremely long blowjob when he tried to watch the game on TV. I swept the tools off his workbench in the basement and bent over it so he could take me from behind. I followed him into the shower when he finished cutting the grass and working in the yard, and when we went to bed that night I was all over him like white on rice. It had the desired effect:

"How soon can you get Mark over here? I need some fucking help."

"Are you sure? It is what I did with Mark that has turned me into a horny slut. If I do it again, it will just reinforce the feeling and I'll be after you even more."

"Maybe, but at least for the time he is here you will be leaving me alone. Besides, getting my fantasy and actually seeing you with another man may just charge me up enough that I can keep up with you.

~~***~~

Monday was a bad day for me. I was as horny as a goat and even though I wanted to call Mark and ask him to come by the house that night, I couldn't. I told him to give me a call in a couple of days and if I called him that would make me seem too eager and would plant ideas in his head that I didn't want him to have. Mark was only going to be a fling, one of many I sincerely hoped, and I did not want him to start thinking of me in terms of a long relationship.

The itch between my legs was so bad that by ten o'clock I was eyeing the men in the office and wondering if I could get away with dragging one of them into the supply closet. It was just a random thought because I knew it was impossibility. The closet was in plain sight of every one in the office and my going into it with a man (if the others figured out what for) would lead to a line forming outside the door. I smiled at that thought. Chuck had said that his fantasy had me servicing men like Randy's wife had and I wondered if he would ever take it that far.

I managed to make it through the day without raping one of my male co-workers. I was driving home and thinking about how poor Chuck's cock might be raw by the time I got done with him that night when my cellphone beeped. I fished it out of my purse and answered it. It was Mark:

"Hi there, you sexy and drop dead gorgeous lady."

"Why thank you sir and just what do you hope to get with that line?"

"To be brutally honest I am hoping for more that just conversation. You told me to call you in a couple of days and I do know that a couple means two and it has only been a day and a half, but if I waited any longer it would be an insult to your beauty."

"Oh God, what a line. Good for a girl's ego though even if it is s line of bull."

"Oh come on, you have to know how much you turned me on the other night. I haven't thought of anything since and I'm on pins and needles waiting to find out if you are going to see me again."

"Look, I'm in my car right now and I don't like talking on my cell when I'm driving. Give me your number and as soon as I can find a place to pull over I'll call you back."

As soon as I had disconnected I called Chuck:

"I just talked to Mark. He's eager, so when do you want to do it?"

"As soon as you can. I can be home by six if tonight is good for you."

"Sweetie, it doesn't matter what is good for me, this is for you, remember?"

"Don't quibble Lorrie, you know you are as turned on by this as I am. I'll bet your pussy is leaking even as we speak."

He was right of course and I told him that I would call Mark back and if that night was good for him I'd set it up and call him right back and let him know. I found a place and pulled over and I already had a finger in my pussy when Mark answered his phone.

"Now where were we?" I said.

"I was trying to convince you to see me again."

"Well I do have to admit that I enjoyed it even though it was in a cramped back seat. I would probably enjoy it even more if it was on a bed, especially if we didn't have to be rushed like we were at the party."

"So, does that mean yes?"

"Not necessarily. Do you remember what I told you? That I was looking for an experience, not a relationship?"

"Yes, I remember."

"That is still true. Even if I do see you again you need to understand that I won't be making a habit of it."

"Is that a yes?"

"That depends on you."

"How?"

"Chuck has a business dinner to attend tonight and won't be home until eleven. If you are free tonight then it is a yes, if you can't make it you will need to chalk it up as another opportunity lost."

"I'll be there. What time?"

"Make it six-thirty. And Mark? Don't forget the condoms – at least four hours worth."

~~***~~

Chuck's car was in the drive when I got home so when I walked into the house I hollered out, "Honey, I'm home."

"I'm upstairs in the bedroom."

I went up and found him rearranging the closet. "I don't know how long I'm going to be in here so I want to make myself as comfortable as I can," he said as he set a folding chair inside. "How long do you think it will take?"

"That is up to you. I told him you wouldn't be home until eleven. I told him to be here at six-thirty so to stay with the story I told him I'll have to get him out of here by ten-thirty. Can you stay in there that long or do you want to give me a time limit?"

"I don't know. I'm new at this."

"Well, so am I sweetie. One night on a back seat doesn't make me an expert. I do know that as horny as I've been since that night on the back seat I can probably go four hours if he can."

"Okay then, how about this. I'll have my cellphone with me and I'll have it set on 'vibrate' so it won't ring while I'm in the closet. If I have to come out, need to come out or am just ready to come out I'll hit the pre-select for the home phone. You answer, hold a fake conversation, and tell him that I finished my meting early and am on the way home."

I looked at my watch. "We have time; want to warm me up for him? Want to give him some sloppy seconds? He has to use a condom, but you don't."

~~***~~

"Damn baby, you sure are wet."

"I've been positively dripping since talking to you on the phone. I can't believe how horny it is making me to be fucking a man who isn't my husband. I'm getting off on being a cheating whore."

"You aren't a whore baby, you are a slut. Whores charge."

"Oh, you sweet talking devil you. Bring that nice black cock over here and let me pretend it is an ice cream cone."

"Why is it every time you mention my cock you refer to it as 'black'?"

"Well, it is, isn't it?"

"Yeah, but why do you always comment on it?"

"Because it is black and until you I have never had anything to do with black men."

"So that is just part of the experience you were looking for?"

"Of course. I've always heard that black men lust after white women and if that is true you need to get over here right now and stop wasting valuable time."

I was sitting so Chuck could see my profile and I hoped that he was enjoying the show as much as I was enjoying giving it to him. I made love to Mark's black pole. I licked it, sucked it and then I deep throated him and hoped had a clear view as inch after black inch disappeared into my mouth. I was an absolute slut! After I swallowed that first load, I kept sucking him until he was hard again and then I laid back and spread myself wide for him. He started to mount me, but I stooped him:

"Forgetting something?"

"What?"

"Where is the protection?"

"Sweetie, you can trust me on this – I don't have any diseases. I like my pussy too much to let that happen to me. Word got out that I had something like that I would be condemned to my fist forever."

"Look baby, I want your hard black cock, but I don't want any black babies. Put a rubber on or say goodnight and leave."

He rolled a condom on and the he fucked me good and hard for almost five minutes before cumming again. I sucked him hard and he fucked me a second time while I kicked, screamed, moaned, cried out and begged him to go harder and faster and to make me cum and make me cum he did. I had orgasm after orgasm as he pounded deep into me. He came and I immediately went down on him again and when I felt him start to rise I got on my hands and knees and told him I wanted him to do me in my ass. I squealed like a pig when Mark slid his hard black cock into my ass and then I begged him to fuck me hard and never stop. I promised him he could have whatever he wanted if he would just fuck me forever.

I got off six times and I got Mark up and off five times before the bedside telephone rang. I glanced at the clock and saw that Chuck had managed to hold on until nine forty-five before having to call. I couldn't resist the chance to be real slutty for Mark. I had been working on Mark's cock trying to get him up one more time when the phone rang and it was halfway stiff and I motioned for him to get behind me and I got up on my knees and answered the phone:

"Hello?"

"Oh, hi sweetie."

Nothing much."

"No, just here waiting for you to get home. I'm horny as hell and I need you."

"What the hell do you think I need you for?"

"That's right sweetie, I need that hard hunk you have. Right now I'm on the bed using my dildo on my pussy. Here, listen."

I held the phone down to my pussy so that Chuck, had he really been on the phone, could hear the 'squish, squish' of Mark's cock sliding in and back in my super hot and thoroughly cum filled pussy.

"Hear that baby? It is already wet for you. Hurry baby, I need your cock."

I hung up the phone and cried, "Hurry Mark, hurry lover, fuck me hard but hurry. He finished his meeting early and he's on his way home. Get me off baby, get me off one more time, but hurry."

Poor Mark. He had already cum five times and there was no way he could hurry along a sixth ejaculation. He was in my hot wet pussy and pounding hard, but he knew he couldn't cum quickly. His big head and little head were fighting each other for control; his big head was telling him to quit, get dressed and get the hell out before Chuck got home and caught his ass, but the little head was screaming:

"Almost there, just another minute, almost there, one more minute, just one more minute."

And then there was me of course:

"Hurry lover, hurry, make me cum baby, one more time, make me cum baby, make me cum."

It was evil of me and I know it, but I wanted to give Chuck a present for letting me do what I was doing and I remembered how angry he had been at Mark for what Mark had done at the first party. I goaded Mark a little more, "Come on lover, come on, hurry, Chuck is on the way, but I need to cum. Faster baby, fuck me faster, hurry baby, hurry, make me cum."

The little head was winning the fight with the big head and he was breathing hard and ramming me hard when suddenly I rolled out from under him and scrambled off the bed. Mark's cock was bobbing up and down and he had a confused look on his face. What had just happened hadn't made its way to the big head yet.

I started grabbing up his clothes and tossing them at him, "I'm sorry lover, I was so close, so close, but Chuck is only minutes away. Hurry lover, you need to get out of here now. Get dressed and go. I need to get this bed straight and get rid of these rubbers and clean myself up a little before Chuck sees me. Hurry Mark hurry. We only have minutes."

Mark got his pants and shirt on and with his shoes, socks, and boxers in his hand he raced for the stairs. He hadn't even opened the front door yet and I was pulling the closet door open and going to my knees in front of my husband. His cock was sticking straight out in front of him and was slick from the juices he had stroked out of himself during his three hours in isolation. His hand was still wrapped around his cock when my mouth closed around it and I grabbed his ass and pulled him to me. I was on him so fast that my chin hit his hand before he could let go. His cock hit the back of my throat and he blew. I held him in my mouth until he was soft and then I stood up and led him to the bed.

"Was it good for you baby? Was it what you wanted, what you expected?"

"Oh sweet Jesus was it ever. You were such a slut with him it was all I could do to keep from coming out of the closet and joining you."

"Why didn't you? I was on a roll; I could have done you and a half dozen more. I was hot baby, I was real hot."

"Half a dozen huh? I just may give you the chance."

~~***~~

Chuck had gotten himself off so many times in the closet that I was only able to get him up twice more that night and after he fell asleep, I lay there looking up at the ceiling and I thought about what Chuck had said when I mentioned a half dozen more. "I just may give you the chance," he'd said. Would he? More to the point, would I if he gave me the chance?

Chapter 4

The next five weeks were glorious from my standpoint. Chuck had been so turned on by watching Mark fuck me that he wanted me to do it again. I had Mark back on Thursday and spent three hours with him while my hubby watched from the closet. As he was getting ready to leave, Mark asked me when he could see me again and that is when I gave him the bad news:

"You can't lover. It has been a blast and I have loved every minute of it, but I told you going in that I wasn't looking for a relationship, just an experience."

Saturday, we went to a party and I let Jack Malloy talk me into going outside for some fresh air. We did some heavy necking and it turned into a grope session with him getting a finger in my pussy and my giving his cock a few strokes. I told him I couldn't do anything there because Chuck was around, but if he wanted to stop by my house on Tuesday when Chuck was at a business meeting maybe we could get something going. I let him have me Tuesday and again on Thursday and then I told him goodbye.

That set the pattern for the coming weeks. A party on Saturday or Sunday to pick out my next lover who got to enjoy me (and me him) on two nights during the coming week and then he was gone and I was looking forward to the next party. Chuck was in a constant state of arousal and I was getting more sex from him in a week than I got in the three months prior to starting our watching arrangement.

There was just one problem – the more cock I got the more I wanted! I spent my days at work wanting cock. I wanted cock in my pussy, cock in my ass and cock in my mouth and some days I didn't want to wait until I could get home to Chuck or my lover of the week. I began to visit the bookstore regularly on my lunch hour. I know I was stretching it, but I didn't believe that I was cheating on Chuck as long as I didn't take a cock in my pussy or ass. Not that I did a lot of cock sucking; it had to be a really nice one for me to do that, but almost every day at lunch some guy got his cock worked on by my hand while I masturbated. One day, I even took a long lunch and jacked off three and sucked off one.

I was out of control and I knew it, but the charge I got out of leaving that booth and walking through a store with several men standing around in it and not having the slightest idea which of them I'd just done was out of sight. It was destructive behavior and only God knows what would have happened to me had I not had an unbelievable stroke of luck. Cathy, one of the girls I work with came up to me just before lunch one day and asked me if I was up for some excitement. It turns out that her brother was a cop and he told Cathy they were going to raid the bookstore that was close to where she worked and that if she just happened to be in the area of 11th and Sutton around twelve-fifteen she could watch it go down.

"Why would they raid an adult bookstore?" I asked.

"Joe says they received a tip that there is a hooker working in the arcade. You want to go with me?"

"It sounds like fun, but I have several errands that I have to run so I'll have to take a pass."

No way was I going to be anywhere that corner. I could just see the cops leading out someone in hand cuffs and have the guy suddenly see me across the street and yell, "There she is, over there, the blonde in the blue coat – that's her!" That put an end to my lunchtime fun, but still left me with the want – the hunger – and no way to do anything about it during the day.

~~***~~

That weekend, Chuck took me to the next step. We were going to a party at the home of one of the guys he worked with. On the drive over Chuck said, "You feel like a change of pace baby?"

"What kind of change?"

"I told you way back at the beginning that my fantasy started out as me watching you with another man, but that it changed into me wanting to see you with several men."

"I remember."

"I'd like to see you do two tonight."

"You want me to take two out to the car?"

"No, not the car. Either during the party or after we will go to a bedroom with Tony and Roy."

"Tony and Roy? I take it from the way you are talking that you won't be in the closet this time?"

"No, this time I get to play too."

"So, we aren't really talking two, we are talking three?"

"Yeah, three of us."

"Jesus Chuck, I don't know about this."

"Why not?"

"I don't know if I can do three. Up till now all I've ever done is one. Doing one is no different than just doing it with you. And I don't know Tony or Roy. Up till now I've only done it with guys I know and feel I can trust to keep their mouths shut."

"Tony and Roy will keep quiet about it. They haven't ever said a word about what they do with Alice at Randy's poker games."

"Are they expecting it to happen?"

"No, they are hoping, but I told them that I hadn't talked with you about it yet. I told them that I thought you might, but I didn't promise."

"Well, I'm not going to promise anything either. We will have to see how things go after I meet them."

~~***~~

I was not going to miss my trips to the adult bookstore. My new problem was going to be keeping myself from spreading myself on my desk at work and taking on all comers. By the time Tony, Roy and Chuck got through with me I was hooked! It was like one long continuous orgasm as the three men took me one after the other for almost three hours. I had a cock in me almost all the time. One would finish and then he would get out of the way and make room for the next. Two men were always standing there and stroking themselves to get hard again while the third was pounding away at my pussy and making me scream. It was the first time in my life that I had a cock in my mouth and one in my pussy at the same time and I loved it. Tony wanted to try my ass while Roy was in my mouth and Chuck was fucking my pussy, but I wasn't quite ready for that yet.

"Maybe next time lover," I told him. And there was going to be a next time – a lot of next times – I would make damned sure of that.

~~***~~

We were no sooner in the car for the ride home when Chuck said:

"What did you think? It sure looked like you enjoyed yourself."

"Is that your way of asking me if I'll do it again?"

"You did seem to have a good time."

"Of course I had a good time, but that doesn't necessarily mean that I want to do it again."

"Why not, as long as you liked it."

"I liked it, but that doesn't mean that I'm not feeling guilty."

"Guilty about what?"

"Have you forgotten all about the vows I took when we got married?"

"Come on baby, that isn't anything to feel guilty over. All of those words just boil down to one thing – that you will be mine until death do us part. Nothing you have done changes that. You are mine and always will be mine and I know it. No matter what we do that won't change. There is something else that's bugging you, what is it?"

"You won't like it."

"How do you know?"

"I know you Chuck, that's how I know."

"You brought it up sweetie, now you have to tell me or it will just bug me and I'll have to bug you until you spill the beans."

"It bothers me that it is all one sided Chuck. Counting tonight I have done eight different guys for you, but so far you haven't even hinted that you might do what I told you my fantasy was."

"What was that?"

"Don't give me that! You know damned well what 'that' is. I want you to eat my pussy while it has cum in it."

"Hey, that isn't my fault. You always made them wear rubbers."

"That's bullshit Chuck and you know it. I didn't say that it had to be another man's cum. I specifically said I wanted you to eat me after you made love to me. I've never made you wear a condom, but you have never even come close to offering to do it."

"Okay, okay, the next time we make love I'll do it."

"No Chuck. I'm pissed that I had to ask so things have changed. I didn't make Tony, Roy or you wear a condom tonight and I'm so full of cum that I slosh when I walk. When we get home I want you to eat me."

"I can't do that. I can't eat your pussy with the cum of two other guys in you."

"No problem Chuck. That is what I expected you to say."

"What does that mean Loretta? I know that tone of voice, what are you going to do?"

"It isn't what I'm going to do Chuck, it is what I'm not going to do any more. I don't get what I want, you don't get what you want."

"That's not fair Loretta. You like doing what I wanted you to do, but I'm not going to like doing what you want."

"How do you know that if you don't even try?"

"I don't have to try it to know I won't like it."

"That isn't the point Chuck. I gave you your fantasy without knowing if I would like it. Hell, I gave it to you not knowing if you would really like it or could handle it. I did what I did for you, not me, but you can't return the favor? Fine, no problem. You can tell your buddies sorry, but the deal is off."

"What do you mean tell my buddies the deal is off?"

"Is that what you think of me Chuck, that I'm just some dumb bimbo? This whole thing got started because of you watching Randy's wife getting gangbanged at that poker party. Start me out small – one guy – to see if I can handle it. Then you move me up to two of your card-playing buddies. Was the next step going to be three or were you just going to set up a poker game and go for it? That is where you have had this thing headed right from the start, your poker playing buddies gang fucking your wife. Well let me tell you something Chuckie baby, it ain't going to fucking happen. You want me to be a slut for you then you had better get down and be a slut for me – a cum slut. You don't go down on me when we get home no dick but yours will ever touch me again and that ain't all of it. From now on anytime I fuck somebody for you, one or fifty, you will clean me out when they are done and that hubby dear, is what you call non-negotiable."

~~***~~

I wasn't worried that I wouldn't be able to do it again. In fact I knew I would be doing it again and my demand that Chuck suck his friend's cum out of me had nothing to do with my having a fantasy and every thing to do with the fact that I was pissed at my husband big time. I had taken a bathroom break and I don't know if it was that my hearing was especially sharp that night, the guys talking too loud and thinking I couldn't hear or the acoustics of the house were just right, but I heard enough to get really pissed at Chuck.

Tony: She going to do it?

Chuck: No problem. I've got her just where I want her.

Roy: No fooling? This is critical to Ben and me. We don't have wives or steady girlfriends and Alice is the only pussy we were getting and now that she is out of commission we are really hurting.

Chuck: Not to worry buddy. I'll have her pulling trains in no time. We will have a poker party at my place in two weeks and Lorrie will wear all of you out.

Tony: Don't let us down Chuck, we're counting on you.

HE has me where HE wants me? HE will have me pulling trains in no time? There wasn't any doubt in my mind that I would do a gangbang at a poker party. I'd known that I was headed there from the start, but HE was giving a guarantee? He was going to pay for that and there was no doubt in my mind but that he would do it. He had promised his buddies and now he had to deliver or become the object of their scorn and derision.

"Come on Lorrie, you can't be serious about this."

"You don't have to, Chuck, it isn't big deal, but don't you ever ask me to give you one of your fantasies again."

Chuck whined about how it wasn't fair, how gross it was to have to do it with other men's stuff in me and that he would make sure that he did it the next time we made love.

"Fine Chuck, you do that. You can consider that as making us even for what I've done for you and we will put all the fantasies out to pasture and never mention them again."

When we were home and upstairs in the bedroom I undressed and said, "I'm going to take a shower and douche, but before I do are you absolutely sure you want me to?"

"Why wouldn't I want you to?"

"Once I've cleaned Tony and Roy off of me and out of me you won't ever see me with another man again."

"Please Lorrie, don't make me do this."

"I'm not making you do anything Chuck. All I'm saying is that to get what you want I have to get what I want and I want it now."

He stood there looking at me and not saying anything so I said, "Fine. Just remember, it was your choice" and I headed for the bathroom. I had just reached the door and had my hand on the doorknob when he said, "Okay, okay, I'll do it."

~~***~~

It started out as a half-hearted attempt to placate me, but I wasn't having any of that. Chuck had stepped into it big time when he said what he said without making sure that I couldn't overhear him and I was not going to let him off easy. As soon as his tongue touched me, I had the fingers of both hands in his hair and I pulled him to my (considering how much man juice he and his buddies had left there) fountain of love. It wasn't about me getting another orgasm, it was simply my getting back at Chuck for what he'd said to Tony and Roy, but as soon as Chuck found my clit he went to work in earnest. He must have decided that since he had to be there anyway he might as well see if he could make me happy. He did. Chuck had eaten my pussy a lot over the years we had been married, but it had always been a foreplay thing; he had never dug in the way he did this time and he actually gave me a very large orgasm. When it was over and I had relaxed and let go of his head he asked:

"Was it what you expected?"

"It was more. You actually ate me to an orgasm. You keep doing that and I'll do a gangbang for you every night of the week."

"You wouldn't say no to a poker party this next Friday?"

"If you eat me like that when it is over I wouldn't say no to a poker party an hour from now."

"So I can go ahead and set it up?"

"How many?"

"Seven, including me."

"Who are they?"

"Just the guys from work."

"Is Alice going to be upset with me for stealing her action?"

"Alice had a hysterectomy last month so the boys haven't done anything but play poker."

"Is this office politics? Are you using me to get on the good side of Randy?"

"No baby, nothing like that. I've wanted to watch you ever since the night I watched Alice."

"Okay lover, bring em on; just remember, I do them and you do your imitation of a Hoover vacuum cleaner when they are done."

Chapter 5

That week I limited myself to Chuck. I wanted to go into that Friday with a sexual hunger that would amaze Chuck's buddies. There was an ego thing going on there also. When I finished with them (or they finished with me) I wanted them all to say, "Alice who?" Chuck wasn't aware of it yet, but if things went well on Friday I planned on pushing him into having poker games every Friday at our house.

As the Friday of the game approached, I spent some time thinking on what had happened between Chuck and I since he had sampled Alice at Randy's poker game. I had become a flaming slut while holding Chuck on a pretty tight rein. I was fucking a new man every week while telling Chuck he had better keep his cock in his pants. I had no idea why I was being that way although I suspected that it had something to do with some sort of insecurity on my part. I think that I felt the real reason that Chuck had for getting me together with other men was so that he could go after other women without fear of reprisal. In the back of my mind was the thought that he wanted to have more fun with Alice.

In the beginning I had told Chuck no more poker games at Randy's, but I ended up backing off on that. Not being one of the guys invited to the game would have an effect on his career and I couldn't do that to him. I told him he could go to the games, but he had better quietly fade away when the game was over. I told him if he even looked in Alice's direction I would neuter him. Now I was starting to have a change of heart. Watching me was obviously turning Chuck on and he was constantly on me to do it again and again. I decided that if the poker game went well I would let him loose so he could go play. What the hell, if he wore himself out with some other slut I'd still have my list of lovers that I could pick a name off of.

~~***~~

The poker party went better than just well. From my standpoint, it was awesome although to be honest I would have liked to have had a few more men there. Two or three more and it might have gone on for another hour or so. If I ever had any doubts that I had become a slut they were dispelled at that party. For the first time in my life, I begged a man to fuck me in my ass. I asked for three men to take me at the same time. I was just shameless.

The plan had been for it to be just like Randy's poker parties; play cards until it was time for the last hand, throw my thong in the pot and then let the games begin. It didn't go that way at all. At Randy's games Alice was never a presence until the end. I didn't intend to go watch TV or read a book until they decided they were ready. I dressed for the occasion in a way that I hoped would light some quick fires. Low cut blouse with no bra, the shortest skirt that I owned, my thong and a pair of Come Fuck Me pumps with a five-inch heel. I didn't wear any nylons because I'd heard that there wasn't anything sluttier than bare legs with high heels.

Chuck called and said he was running a little late and I should make the guys comfortable and give them drinks and snacks until he got there. When Tony arrived, I gave him a kiss with a little tongue, squeezed his crotch and said, "Still want to try my ass out lover?"

I did the same thing to Roy when he got there so I knew at least those two wouldn't have their minds on there cards. Randy was the last to show up and he took the time to look me up and down and then he said:

"If you are half as good as you look we are going to be great friends."

"Want a taste right now before the game starts?"

"How come I never knew you were this big of a slut? Why has Chuck been hiding you?"

"I'm a newly minted slut sugar; it has been less than two months since I found out how much fun it could be."

While we were talking, Randy had been unzipping his fly and he pulled out his already hardening cock and I went to my knees in front of him. I was sucking his cock one foot inside my front door before he had even been in my house a full minute. I had his cock pushing at the back of my throat and I had his balls in one hand when I felt someone behind me. My skirt was lifted up and I heard Tony say, "Is this babe ready or what?" and then his hands grabbed my hips and I felt his cock poke at my pussy. I pushed back at him; his cock popped into me and then my world just became one hard cock after another in whichever hole they preferred.

Chuck came home and found us all not at the card table, but upstairs in the bedroom. When he walked through the bedroom doorway, I was sliding up and down on Steve's cock while Tony was taking my ass from the rear and I was just leaning forward to wrap my lips around Mike. I saw Chuck, smiled at him and said, "You told me to take care of them," and then I took Mike's dick in my mouth.

Chuck seemed a little put off by what he had walked in on and he seemed a little shook over the fact that Randy was standing off to the side videotaping the action. Whatever he was going to say, he thought better of and just started undressing. My husband had the unique experience that night of fucking me in all three of my holes while the other two were also occupied. I sucked his cock while Randy was in my pussy and Roy was in my ass. He fucked my pussy while Ben stuffed my pooper and I sucked off Tony and he had my ass while I licked Mike's dick and slid up and down on Harry's.

It was over too soon for me – way too soon, but what's a girl to do when the cocks just won't get hard again? I was at the front door when they all left and I gave each one of them a scorcher of a kiss as I wished them a goodnight. Randy was the last one to leave and after I kissed him he said, "When can we do this again?"

"We can go back upstairs now if you would like."

He laughed, "Bitch. You know I can't get it up anymore tonight."

"Then I guess you will have to discuss it with my social secretary," and I pointed at Chuck.

"See you Monday buddy," he said to Chuck, "And keep her calendar clear."

As soon as the door closed behind Randy I got my first indication that all was not well in paradise. "Why did you do that?" Chuck asked.

"Do what?"

"Invite him back upstairs."

"It's what he came here for isn't it?"

"We were supposed to play cards, not fuck all night."

"Well then, you should have made damned sure you were here when your guests started arriving. Randy wanted to get right to it and there wasn't anyway I was going to put your boss off, especially since you offered me up to them on a platter."

"Why was he videotaping you?"

"You'll have to ask him."

"I'm not happy about the way this went."

"I'm sorry you aren't happy sweetie, but I didn't have a whole lot of control over things once Randy got here and took charge. I was not; repeat not, going to jeopardize your relationship with him by saying no to anything he wanted. He was here by your invitation to fuck your wife and don't you forget that. Now, let's go upstairs so I can get mine."

"What are you talking about?"

"You know damned well what I'm talking about. I made it clear the night I did Tony and Roy for you. I do who you want and then you play vacuum cleaner. Let's go."

"I don't feel like it tonight."

"No problem, just remember that when Randy asks you on Monday when we can do it again that the answer is never. I'm going to bed," I said and I headed for the stairs.

"Damn it Lorrie, this just isn't right. I don't want to do it and you know it, but my career will be in the toilet if I tell Randy no on Monday."

"Tough shit Chuck. I made it plain to you what the price would be before you set this up. If you didn't want to pay that price all you had to do was not have the party. Goodnight," and I again turned and headed for the stairs.

"Damn it Lorrie, you can't do this to me."

"I'm not doing anything to you Chuck, I'm just holding you to your agreement. I do A and in return you do B. I do A and you don't do B then I don't do A anymore. You agreed to that remember? This is all on you Chuck," and I turned and this time I kept walking when he started to whine.

I had him by the balls and I knew it. It was mean as hell of me and I knew that too, but if he was going to use me I was going to use him. I loved the asshole, but I still remembered that "I've got her right where I want her" and the "Don't worry, I'll have her pulling trains in no time." He had to pay for that and the payment had to be something that he didn't want to do. It could have been anything, but eating my cum filled pussy just happened to be it.

When I got to the bedroom I stripped and went and got out my douche bag and headed for the bathroom. I wasn't going to do it, but I had to look like I was ready to when Chuck came into the room. I knew that by the time I hit the top of the stairs he would have worked it through in his mind. Right now he was one of Randy's butt boys, but that would all change Monday when he told Randy that I wasn't going to put out any more. He came into the room and saw me getting ready to douche and I saw the panic on his face.

"Don't Loretta, don't do it. You win. Please, come on to bed."

I couldn't resist one little dig, "Never mind Chuck, you don't really want to do it and I'm not really that certain I want to do Randy and the boys again anyway."

"Damn it Lorrie, you are driving me fucking crazy. Will you please put down that nozzle and come to bed?"

Like the first time he started out slow, but then he got into it and started sucking on my clit and finger fucking my asshole and he brought me off twice before I pushed him away and got into a sixty-nine with him. Wonder of wonders, the cock I couldn't get hard a half-hour ago was standing tall and I swung over him and slid down on him and then I fucked him until he fell asleep.

~~***~~

I was not surprised in the least when Chuck came home from work on Monday and said that Randy wanted to know if I would do another card party. Alice was ready to try again, but Randy didn't know if she would be able to jump back in and go full speed ahead. Randy wanted me there to help out. The honest answer would have been "Hell no! The seven of you didn't give me all I wanted on Friday night, so no way I want to share you with Alice." But of course I couldn't say that. Even if I had to share with Alice I wanted to go play, but I also had to keep it being Chuck's idea so I had to make him ask me.

"I don't know baby. I wonder if maybe we are jumping into this a little too fast. I'm still worried about the reputation I might get if these guys blab it around what I'm doing with them."

"I told you that you don't need to worry about that. These guys have been doing Alice for years and they have never said a word."

"Alice is the bosses wife sweetie. If they talk about her and Randy finds out they are out of a job. I'm just another round-heeled slut to them. They talk about me and you get pissed they can just laugh at you. And then there is the other problem."

"What other problem?"

"The fact that I have to ask you to live up to your part of the bargain every time I do it. Not only do I have to ask, but also I have to threaten you to get you to do it. That isn't any way to keep a marriage going."

"No more babe. You won't ever have to ask me again, I promise."

"Are you sure that you can be comfortable with your co-workers knowing that your wife is a cock crazy whore?"

"Don't be silly Lorrie, you aren't a cock crazy whore."

"Of course, I am Chuck. I don't start out that way, but once they get me going I am. You've seen it with everyone I've put out for since we started doing this. Once I get going you could line up fifty guys and I'd just fuck until I wore them out or they wore me out."

"I'll never do that to you babe. The guys at the card party are the most I'll ever ask you to do."

"You sure that you want me to do it?"

"Yeah Lorrie, I'm sure."

~~***~~

I had a good time, but I didn't get as much as I wanted. I did get more than I thought I would because it turned out that Alice was nowhere near ready. She pooped out after doing four and then she just sat back and watched me be the fuck pig that I turned into once cocks started slamming into my three holes. It went on for hours and when it was over Alice thanked me for being there to help her out and she told me that she hoped we could do it again.

"Tonight showed me that I have a ways to go to come back from my surgery. I can use all the help you can give me."

I didn't know it at the time but when I walked out her front door that night the clock started ticking on the end of my marriage. True to his word I did not have to ask Chuck to clean me out. As soon as we were in the car he pushed me down on the seat and buried his face in my bush. He slurped up the cum deposits of seven men, most of whom had been in my pussy at least three times that night and then we drove home.

~~***~~

I didn't know that we had a problem until Wednesday of the following week. When Chuck came home from work Monday, he seemed strangely quiet and when I asked him if he was all right he told me he had a problem at work that was bothering him. Tuesday was no different and neither was Wednesday so on Wednesday I pushed him on it. It turned out that Harry and Mike had walked by our car on their way to theirs and they had seen Chuck going down on me. On Monday, they started razing him about sucking their cocks by proxy. All Chuck could do was grin and shrug it off and hope it would go away, but of course it didn't.

Harry and Mike told the other guys and they started hacking on Chuck too. I'm sure that it was just joking, but Chuck didn't take it that way. Then Randy told Alice and Alice told him that she would like him to do that for her and he refused so she told him to get Chuck to do it at the next poker game. Randy told Chuck what Alice wanted and said he could do it at the next poker game – didn't ask, just told Chuck to do it at the next game. That left Chuck with the option of saying that of course he would do it and staying in Randy's good graces or saying no and facing the consequences.

Now, he not only had to worry about Randy, but he still had all the other guys doing their 'cocksucker' jokes with Chuck being the butt of them. He tried to put off saying anything to Randy by saying that I had some family things that I had to do for the next couple of months and that we probably wouldn't be attending any games for a while. I don't know how Randy took it, but it made me mad. I was looking forward to the next poker game. Just taking a temporary lover during the week just didn't get it any more. I didn't need just one cock, I needed bunches and there were six besides Chuck's at that game.

The pressure from Randy wasn't the only pressure. I got a call from Alice and it was obvious from the way the conversation went that she recognized me as a kindred spirit and she was going to try and use that to get what she wanted.

"I wanted to thank you again for helping me the other night."

"Believe me, I enjoyed the hell out of it. I understand from Chuck that Randy wants to it again soon."

"Actually we were hoping that you could join us this coming Friday evening, but I understand that you won't be able to make it and that's too bad."

"Why is that?"

"I was so looking forward to talking with you privately about what you and Chuck did after you left the house last Friday."

"Oh? What about it?"

"Not over the phone dear. Any chance you could swing by the house for coffee this afternoon?"

"I don't get off work until five, but I suppose I could stop by on the way home."

"That would be lovely. I do so look forward to seeing you."

~~***~~

I was sitting across the kitchen table from her and sipping a glass of white wine as she explained why she had asked me over.

"It is all I have been able to think about since Randy told me about it. I think about it so much that for the first time in years I've masturbated while imaging it happening. I was in the bathtub this morning relaxing in the hot water and thinking about being eaten after a gangbang and I gave myself a massive orgasm. I just have to do it."

"What has this got to do with me?"

"I need you to convince your husband to do it to me."

"He won't. He fights me on it most of the time. He only does it for me because I tell him I'll stop fucking other men if he doesn't."

"I don't understand."

"His fantasy was to see me with other men – lots of other men – and I suppose I have you to thank for that since it only started happening after his first poker party here. He saw you do everybody and he thought it was neat and he started after me to do it. My price for giving him what he wants is his giving me what I want. Can't you get Randy to do it?"

"No, he flat refuses, says it isn't manly. I've even called the rest of the guys who come to the games to see if one of them would do it. I even offered to spend an entire weekend with Mike if he would do it and they all refused. Your husband is the only one I know who does it. I want you to get him to do it for me."

"I'm sorry Alice, but I can't."

"There is a reason I asked you to come over and talk to me in person rather than on the phone. When you make threats on the phone the other person can hang up."

"Threats?"

"That's right dear. I don't like doing it, but I want my pussy eaten after a gangbang. Chuck is the only candidate and I need you to work on him until he agrees to do it. Chuck has a future with the company, but only if he stays on the right side of Randy and I have a ton of influence with Randy. I can see to it that Chuck is made a vice president or I can see to it that he becomes unemployed and with ghastly references."

Not being stupid I knew that she had Chuck pretty much by the gonads and she was trying to enlist me in helping him to see the light.

"It won't be all one sided Loretta. You help me and I'll help you."

"How? In what way?"

"From what you have told me you are new at this. Have you had your first black experience yet? Your first Latino or Asian?"

"I've had a black man, but not the others."

"I can help you there. In fact, if you would like I can arrange for your first Latino," and she looked at her watch, "In about twenty minutes. Would you like that?"

"In twenty minutes?"

"Yes, I have three of them coming over. In addition to the poker games I help Randy with keeping some of his customers happy. I'll share if you would like."

"It is an intriguing thought, but not this time. My deal with Chuck is based on his wanting me to do it and his being able to watch. Without his involvement it would be cheating and I just can't do that."

"Pity, but you should talk to him about it. As long as you are fucking for him anyway you might as well help him with customers and contracts and have a good time doing it. I trust you will have a nice talk with him tonight about what we have talked about. I do hope to see both of you again soon."

~~***~~

Chuck was in a sour mood when I got home that night. Randy was keeping up the pressure on him to do Alice 'the favor' and he had finally lost it when he and Harry had been in the bathroom together. Harry was at the urinal next to Chuck and they were both peeing. When they were done Harry gave his dick a couple of shakes and then had said to Chuck, "How about it guy. Were alone and I've already have it out." Chuck had broken Harry's nose and had probably bruised or broken a rib when he had worked Harry over. Randy had taken him in the office and asked what the hell had happened and Chuck told him the story. Randy said he didn't want any more violence in the work place:

"One of them might get in a lucky punch and hurt you. I'm not sure that Alice would forgive me if I let that happen. She is looking forward to seeing you again."

Next, Randy called all the guys in the office and told them to knock off the bullshit. "Harry is going to be out for several days and I don't need to lose any more of you."

Ben laughed and said, "No problem boss. We can handle him, right guys?" and Randy had replied "Maybe so, but can you handle him and me?"

Chuck finished telling me about his day, "The guys are probably off my back now, but Randy is still expecting me to do Alice."

"Well, given the day you have just had this probably isn't the best time to bring this up, but then I don't any time would be a good time" and I told him about my visit with Alice."

"Shit! This just gets worse and worse. What the hell am I going to do?"

"The smart move would to become a vice president."

"What does that mean?"

"Alice says she can make you one. If I were you I'd take her up on it and I'd do it soon. We can always tell Randy we cancelled our plans because we would rather be with him and Alice."

"But I don't want to eat her pussy after she has been gang fucked."

"You didn't want to eat mine either, but you did and it didn't kill you."

"Damn it Loretta, you never used to be like this. What the hell has gotten into you?"

"A whole lot of cocks that aren't yours and I'm learning to like it. I almost took Alice up on her invitation to stay and play."

"Why didn't you?"

"Because you weren't there so you could watch. That's what this is all about, remember? You have to be involved or it is no different than cheating."

"You should have called me. I know who visited Alice today and they are some of our very best customers. The way I'm feeling right now I'd rather have you fucking our good customers than my asshole poker buddies."

"But you wouldn't be there to watch."

"Doesn't matter, I'd know about it and if I know about it and have given my approval it isn't cheating."

"You don't care? Just go ahead Loretta, fuck your little head off as long as long as you tell me?"

"Come off of it Lorrie, I wasn't born yesterday. You are loving the hell out of what you are doing and you are only using me as an excuse to do it."

"That's not true sweetie. It is true that I'm loving it, but I do love you and I don't want to screw up our marriage. I'm not using you as an excuse; I'm using you as my anchor. You say stop and no matter how much fun I'm having I'll stop. That said, I don't intend to stop until you tell me to. I'll fuck your poker buddies, your boss, friends I pick up at parties and yes, I'll fuck your customers for you and love doing it, but it has to be because you want me to. Are we clear on that?"

"Yes, I guess we are."

"So the question now is, 'Do you want to be a vice president?'"

Chapter 6

I called Alice and told her our plans had changed and that Chuck and I would see her on Friday.

"Were you able to convince him to do what we talked about?"

"He was very reluctant, but when I told him you would make him a VP he decided that he would do it."

"He does understand that it isn't going to happen over night?"

"I don't know what he thinks about it. That is a discussion that you will have to have with him. Basically I gave him a promise on your behalf that if he does A you will do B so the mechanics of it are up to the two of you."

"Well honey, I will get him there, but it will take a little time. I could maybe hurry it along with some help from you."

"In what way?"

"If you could see your way clear to help me out when things like yesterday come up it would help."

"We talked about that and he is okay with it as long as he knows about it."

"You doing anything tomorrow around three?"

"I have some meetings that I have to attend, but I should be free after two."

"I have four coming to pay me a visit if you would like to give me a hand."

"I'll have to clear it with Chuck, but after our talk last night I don't think it will be a problem."

"Well, call me as soon as you know."

I hung up the phone, took a deep breath and picked it up again. When Chuck answered I said, "Hi lover, your loving slut needs to clear something with you."

"What would that be?"

"I just got off the phone with Alice and she invited me over to help her out with some visiting firemen tomorrow. I told her I would love to but that I needed call and get your okay and I'd call her back."

"I already told you that you could as long as I know about it."

"That isn't the way it works honey bunny. You have to either ask me or tell me before I can do it."

"You lost me there."

"If I go into a bar on Seventh and a guy hits on me and I decided I'd like to go to a motel with him I'm going to call you and ask you if it is all right. If you say no I won't go.   I'm not going to do it and then come home and say, 'Guess what I did today.' With the poker game you asked me to do it, in the bar example you have to tell me it is okay. So, I'm asking if you mind my going over to help Alice tomorrow. I told her I would check with you and call her right back."

"Well Loretta, I'd say that it depends on you."

"How is that?"

"I'm not telling you that you should do it and I'm not asking you to do it. As I understand this conversation you are simply asking if it is okay. Am I right?"

"Yes, that about sums it up."

"Okay then, by saying that I don't mind if you do I am not putting myself in a position where I have to eat your pussy when you are done. As long as we are clear on that feel free to visit Alice tomorrow."

"But I like the way you eat my pussy."

"And I love doing it when it is only me in there, but I'm not all that fond of the taste of others."

"Oh pooh, you're no fun at all."

"Oh I don't know about that. I'll have to see if I can't show you a fun time when I get home tonight."

~~***~~

When I arrived at Alice's home, she met me at the door wearing a bathrobe. "Oh good, you're here," and she took me by the hand and led me out to the patio. I found four black men sitting around the pool in bathing trunks. Alice introduced me and said, "We have just been waiting for you dear and she dropped the robe and I saw that she was naked underneath.

"How about it boys, ready to take this party to the bedroom?"

The next four hours were extremely enjoyable and I did have a great time, but when it was over and Alice asked me if I'd liked it I told her the truth:

"I enjoyed it, but I was a little disappointed."

"Why is that?"

"Ever since I started high school I heard about how all blacks had huge cocks and how if you once made love with one of them you would be spoiled for life. My first black man was no bigger than Chuck and wasn't as good a lover and I thought he just might have been the exception that proved the rule. So today I tried four more and I guess it is a little bit of a let down to find out that they are all just normal guys."

"If a huge cock is what you want honey, I'll call you the next time Fred Guinn comes to town and let you take care of him."

"I wasn't asking for a big one Alice, all I said was that from what I'd heard I'd expected more. Got to run. I need to get home and get Chuck's dinner on. See you Friday."

~~***~~

Dinner was on the table when Chuck got home. I greeted with a kiss and I wondered if he could taste any of what made it into my mouth that afternoon. Sluttish of me and I knew it, but that was what this was all about wasn't it? I'd become a slut for my husband. I was leaving parties and going out to back seats with guys, I was pulling trains at poker parties and I'd just added servicing the customers of my husband's company. Add to that, regardless of what I'd told Alice, I was all ready wondering about the size of Fred Guinn's cock and if I could handle it.

I made the kiss a passionate one and dropped a hand to squeeze Chuck's cock through his trousers, "Dinner is ready baby, but even though I've slaved over a hot stove for you I will understand if you decide that you would rather have dessert first."

"And just what are you offering for dessert?"

"What I would really, really like is to give you some cream pie followed by a long session of trying to fuck your brains out."

"What's the matter, you didn't get enough this afternoon?"

"I never seem to get enough any more. Ever since we started giving you your fantasy the more I get, the more I seem to want. Come on lover, let's go do dessert."

Chuck followed me up the stairs and on the way to the bedroom I kept working on him to eat my pussy and he kept saying that he didn't feel like it. Finally I begged him:

"Please baby, please? You know how much I love it so please do it for me, please?"

He said okay and he went to work on me half-heartedly until I started screaming and pushing my pussy up at his face and grabbed the back of his head as I had an orgasm. He must have decided to see just how much more he could make me scream and cum and he went to work and put some effort into it. He sucked and licked and worked my clit and I had two more orgasms. The two were so close together that they almost seemed like one long one and I would have loved to stay there and let Chuck keep doing what he was doing, but I had promised to fuck his brains out. I needed to do my best to keep him happy so he wouldn't decide to put an end to what we were doing.

I started to wear him out and I did. Each time he came I immediately went down on him until I had him ready again and then we started all over. He finally pushed me away:

"Enough already! You have to leave me enough strength to get out of bed and go to work in the morning."

"Oh I don't know about that. You do a really good job on Alice this Friday and you may never have to go to the office again."

Just then the phone rang and Chuck answered it:

"Speak of the devil," he said as he handed me the phone.

"Hello?

"Hello yourself you beautiful slut. Chuck sounded a bit out of breath, did I interrupt anything?"

"Not really. I promised him if he would eat my pussy I would fuck his brains out and he just cried uncle so I think I lived up to my promise."

"Oh you slut you. Did you douche first or did he suck up all the stuff those niggers left in you?"

I felt a little chill when she said 'niggers' in the tone of voice she used and I said, "Is that not a good thing?"

"I don't know sweetie; I don't know Chuck that well, but with Randy I have to be very careful. Even though he is the one setting me up with them I don't dare let him know that I'm enjoying myself and having a good time. I have to tell Randy that I was acting when a black customer tells him that he had a good time."

"I should be okay since Chuck knows."

"He does? That's cool and kind of a good thing since that is why I'm calling you."

"Oh? What's up?"

"You remember Bob from this afternoon?"

"The one with the goatee, right?"

"Yes. Well, he is from out of town and doesn't know anyone here. He needs a date for an awards dinner he is attending tomorrow night. It is a political thing and his stock will go up if his date is a beautiful white woman. He called Randy to see if I would do it, but I already have something going for tomorrow. Then he asked Randy for your phone number. Randy called me and asked me to call you and sound you out on it. He wanted to know how you felt about it before he approached Chuck on the deal. It is pretty important sweetie. He still hasn't signed the contract and his business is worth just a little over two million a year to the company."

"Does this fall under the category of helping speed things along as far as VP goes?"

"Oh most definitely slut sister, most definitely."

"I do this and he signs and Chuck gets full credit, right?"

"I wouldn't let it go any other way sweetie."

"Tomorrow is Chuck's lodge meeting so I'm free. Call me in the morning with the details."

"You sure you don't want Randy to handle it through Chuck?"

"No, I think we have it covered."

When I hung up Chuck asked me what it was all about and I told him.

"That's it? Sure Alice, count me in. I don't even get a voice in this?"

"Of course you have a voice in it. You already told me I could work with Alice on this kind of thing and that all I had to do was make sure that you knew about it. You won't be home tomorrow night so I said yes. It's a two million-dollar deal and you get full credit for it. It is up to you baby. I can call Alice back and cancel on it if that is what you want."

"No, not now. By now, she's told Randy and he is probably all ready on the phone to Bob. But next time keep me in the loop okay? Humor me a little. Let me pretend that I count for something around here," and then he rolled over and didn't even kiss me goodnight.

~~***~~

I lay awake and stared up at the ceiling for a long time that night and thought about a lot of things including the abrupt way that Chuck had ended the evening. A lot of it had to do with the way Alice had said 'niggers' when she talked to me and the fact that I had Chuck eat my pussy wile it was still full of an afternoons worth of cum from black men. I told Alice that Chuck knew it when he went down on me, but did he really? The day I had come home from visiting Alice and hearing her threat Chuck told me that he knew who was going to be with Alice that day. I assumed that he knew who I'd been with that afternoon. What if he didn't? I'd never heard Chuck make a racial remark, but what if he felt like Randy did? Then I thought no, he knows who Bob is and he knows that I'll probably end up in bed with him before the date is over and he didn't say anything. Then again, he did give me the cold shoulder, roll over and go to sleep without kissing me goodnight.

Then a really bad thought hit me. Would Alice tell Randy that Chuck ate my pussy after four black men played around in it that afternoon? Would the other guys find out? Would they start ragging on Chuck again? I was still thinking about all that stuff when I finally fell asleep.

~~***~~

My date with Bob started out just as most first dates I'd had when I was still single. He picked me up at six-thirty and we made polite conversation on the drive to where the awards dinner was being held. We talked about the weather, raising kids; the high price of gasoline and about almost everything except about what we both knew was going to happen. I was pleased to see when I glanced at his lap that he was thinking of me. Just before we got out of the car to go inside, he asked me what time he had to have me home and I told him that I needed to get home in time to get my husband off to work and my kids off to school. He raised an eyebrow at that, but didn't say anything.

Once inside I received a surprise. Not only was I the only white, I was also the only woman and I commented on that to Bob.

"That's why I wanted you or Alice to be here with me tonight. The rule is a white woman or no woman at all. Regardless of all you hear about white women lusting after black men it is not really all that easy for a man of my race to date a white woman. My standing in this group just got a whole lot higher. It is an ego thing."

"I don't understand. I see mixed couples around all the time."

"Yes, and those are probably established relationships that took a long time to form. I'm talking about calling a white woman and asking for a first date. Not all that easy, believe me. All I need you to do is be just what you were in the car. A white housewife who just happens to have a taste for a little extracurricular activity with a black man. Just be your normal self around these guys. One other thing. You will be hit on a lot tonight and after the dinner and the awards ceremony is over, we will go up to the hospitality suite for the cocktail party and you can play all you want, but until then please just smile and say you are with me."

I smiled at him, "I am with you sweetie. I'm with you until you take me home. If I play with anyone else but you it will only be after they ask you and you say it is okay."

Bob did say it was okay and he said it to quite a few people. Dinner was prime rib and by the time the awards ceremony was over (Bob didn't win anything, but then he had me, right?) and I'd had a few drinks, I was ready. Every time Bob walked away from me to get fresh drinks or to use the john some guy would try and move in on me. I got felt up, had my hands placed on hard lumps and in one instance a guy even took his cock out to show it to me.

"What do you think of this one toots? Ever seen one so big and so nice?"

As a matter of fact, I had and I almost laughed at the guy and said, "Yes I have, hanging between my husband's legs" but this was Bob's party and I had no idea who the guy was so I just said, "Ooh, I would like to try one like that some day."

He saw Bob coming back so he tucked his dick back in his pants and moved away. By the time we moved to the hospitality suite I was hot and ready to fuck and I told Bob and asked:

"Are we going to find a bed somewhere?"

He looked at me with an amused look on his face, "You aren't doing this just to get my business are you? You want to do this right?"

"Let's be straight on this lover. Randy and my husband want a signed contract and for my own piece of mind, at least where my husband is concerned, I would dearly love to hand it to them. But if you had called me direct instead of going through Alice or Randy and had asked me to be your date tonight and no contracts had been mentioned I still would have said yes. And before you ask, yes I do love my husband, but I need more sex than any one man can give me. My husband knows this about me and because he loves me he lets me play."

"More than any one man can give you? Well baby, the one thing I don't like to do is disappoint my ladies."

~~***~~

I had fourteen men that night, most more than once and more than a couple of times I had three in me. At one point during the evening I actually called out "next" when one man came in my mouth and pulled out. Then Bob took me to his hotel room where we made love twice before falling asleep. He woke me up at five-thirty and as he was driving me home he asked me if I'd gotten enough and I giggled and told him that I'd had enough to hold me until my hubby got home from work that evening.

"May I call you the next time I come to town?"

"I would be disappointed if you didn't."

He drove off and I hoped that the neighbors didn't notice the way I was walking as I headed for my front door. And yes, Bob did sign the contract, which moved Chuck one step closer to becoming a vice president.

~~***~~

What I didn't realize at the time was that while my evening with Bob had gotten the contract that moved Chuck one step closer to being a vice president, it also moved our marriage one step closer to being over. Bob had given me a glowing recommendation to Randy and it got Randy to thinking that I could do him some good in other areas. Specifically, he had a ton of customers he thought might like a taste of me. I started getting more and more calls from Alice to help her out. Over the next two months I got to sample a mini United Nations. Asians, Latinos, blacks, Arabs and mixtures I couldn't even begin to describe climbed on my body and fucked me until I was exhausted.

I was loving it and hoping that it would never end and Chuck was bringing home enormous bonus and commission checks. In addition there were still the Friday night poker games and they had gone from once every two weeks to weekly and they rotated between our house and Randy's. Chuck did go down on Alice and eat her after she had been gangbanged by the guys and she had gone wild. Chuck ate Alice while I sucked his cock and Randy fucked me, and then Chuck ate me while Randy fucked Alice and then Chuck ate her again. It was a very enjoyable night, but it was also another step toward the end of our marriage.

The last step on the road to the end of our marriage came on a Tuesday night in June. Chuck had been promoted to vice president and Randy had sent him out of town to close a deal with a supplier. I drove Chuck to the airport and dropped him off and when I got home I walked into the house just as the phone rang. It was Randy and he had a problem.

"I know it is real short notice but I have some clients who just came to town and Alice is going to need some help. Are you up for it?"

"Sure. Just give me a chance to take a quick shower and dress sexy."

I got myself ready and headed on over to Randy's house. There were nine guys there and I was no sooner in the door than my clothes were being peeled off of me. It was two in the morning before things broke up and then Randy asked me if I would mind going back to the hotel with one of the men. I said okay and I went with the guy, his name was Sean, to his room. We had a couple of drinks and then climbed on the bed. He was pounding me in the butt when the door to the room opened and another guy came in. It turned out that Sean was sharing the room with the guy and so they decided to share me. Somewhere along the way, three other guys stopped by and it was six in the morning before I finally told them I had to end it so I could get home.

When I got home the message machine had several calls from Chuck on it and with each call he seemed angrier and angrier. I tried calling Chuck, but couldn't get in touch with him. I tried calling him from work with no luck. That evening while I was fixing myself some dinner, Chuck called. I answered the phone, said hello, and he said:

"Where in the fuck have you been?"

I hung up on him and a minute later it rang again and I answered it and my hello got:

"Don't you fucking dare hang up on me," and I hung up on him again. The third time it rang I picked up the phone and said:

"You have reached the telephone answering machine of Chuck and Loretta Barlow. If you would like to hold a civil conversation please press one. If you wish to be a belligerent asshole press two and this machine will disconnect the call."

There was silence on the other end and then, "Where have you been Loretta?"

I told him about Randy calling me the night before and then I told him how the night had gone.

"I told him that I didn't want him or Alice calling you anymore."

"You never told me that and if I don't know why would I say no to either Randy or Alice when they call?"

"Okay, okay, you're right. I should have let you know. But you know now. I don't want you to do it any more."

"Why? What has happened?"

"We can talk about it when I get home. I'm late for a meeting and I have to run. Just remember, if Alice or Randy call you aren't available."

Well, neither Alice nor Randy called, but Bob did. He was in town and could I have dinner with him. I knew deep down I should have said no, but I started rationalizing. Bob's business was worth two million a year to Chuck's company and I had been instrumental in getting Bob's business. Not knowing what was going on should I keep Bob happy until I found out or say no, sorry, but I can't. I told him I'd have to make a call and I'd get back to him. I tried calling Chuck, but he didn't answer. I decided to err on the side of caution so I called Bob back and told him I could do it. Bob and I went out to dinner. Of course, we ended up in his hotel room and I drained him dry.

"You need more?" he asked while I was unsuccessfully trying to get him up again and I told him I always needed more. He picked up the phone and thirty minutes later I had a cock in all three of my love nests. It was two in the morning when I got home and the telephone answering machine had four calls from Chuck and they got increasingly belligerent as I went through them.

Well, I couldn't say that I didn't expect it. Chuck's call came while I was fixing myself breakfast. He started out with a calm:

"Where were you when I called?"

I told him and he got angry.

"What the fuck is wrong with you Loretta? Are you doing all of your thinking with your cunt now?"

"Don't you dare give me that shit, Chuck! It was you thinking with your dick that got us started down this road. You wouldn't tell me what was going on when we talked yesterday, all you did was tell me not to take calls from Randy or Alice. Bob is your account and is worth two million a year to your company. I tried calling you, but you didn't answer your phone. No way I'm going to say no to him and jeopardize the account for you until I know what the hell is going on. If I had said no and you lost the account you would be screaming at me about that now instead of giving me shit because I tried to keep things cool until you got home and we could talk."

"Bullshit Loretta. What really is going on is that you have become a cock crazy whore."

"Oh, is that so. Well in that case you can cab home from the airport. Instead of picking you up the cock crazy whore is going to go out and find herself some cock!" and I slammed the phone down. It rang a minute later and I ignored it.

Alice called me at work around eleven and asked me if I could have lunch with a couple of guys from Ajax Chemicals and I told her I couldn't and then I told her about my calls from Chuck.

"That goddamned fuckhead!"

"What?"

"Oh no honey, not Chuck; that idiot I'm married to is the fuckhead."

"I don't understand."

"Come on over honey; we can have coffee and talk."

~~***~~

"Lorrie, I'm a slut," Alice said, "And I've never tried to hide it or pretend otherwise. I think the reason I took to you right away is that I recognized one of my own kind. As a slut I do slutty things and three weeks ago Randy had several of our very good customers over and while I was doing my best to fuck them all to death Randy was showing videos of me doing what I do best. The asshole knew better and I made him promise that no one would ever see them, but he slipped in the tape of Chuck taking turns at eating us out after the poker game.

"Randy can make the guys in the office behave, but he can't do anything about our customers and a couple of the ones Chuck deals with started getting on him. It was all good-natured kidding, but Chuck is apparently very sensitive when it comes to that. He stormed into Randy's office and they almost came to blows over it. Randy called me and told me he was going to fire Chuck and I told him that if he did I'd cut him off and that all he would ever get of me again was being able to watch me fuck our customers. Anyway, the relationship between Chuck and Randy hasn't been of the best lately, but I didn't know that it had carried over to you."

"So Chuck has one foot out the door and one foot on a banana peel and he knows it? And since he knows he's history anyway he is telling me to tell you to go fly a kite?"

"It might seem that way to him honey, but it isn't that way at all. He isn't going anywhere unless he chooses to do so on his own. I made Chuck a vice president because he earned it and I don't mean he earned it by eating my pussy. My threat that day was an empty one honey. If you would have to me to fuck off and die I still would have made Chuck a VP."

"That's you, but Chuck has to deal with Randy."

"Yes and no."

"What does that mean?"

"I own the company honey. It was my father's and he left it to me. I put Randy in as president because he was my husband, but I run the company. I won't say this to Randy, or Chuck for that matter, but Chuck has more ability in his little finger than Randy has in his whole body. I love the big doofus, but I'm not blind to his faults. Chuck is being groomed to take over from Randy when I finally decide it is time for him to retire to a life of leisure. I would appreciate it if you would keep that to yourself. The last thing I need is for Chuck to start looking smug around Randy. As far as Chuck's slurping pussy is concerned, he will just have to find some way to deal with it. I just hope he doesn't stop doing me. Feel better now that things are clear?"

"No, not really. I think Chuck is going to quit. He may punch Randy out before he does and the only way I can stop that is to tell him what you have just told me. Even then I think Chuck plans on telling me to stop being the slut I've come to love being and I don't know that I can stop. I do know that I won't sneak around if I do decide to keep on doing it and that won't set well with Chuck, not at all. Long term I'll just have to see. Short term I'm going to take what I can get. Think the boys from Ajax might still be interested in some company?"

~~***~~

They were and they had a friend who had a friend and when I got home Chuck was sitting at the kitchen table sipping a beer and fuming. He looked at me and snarled:

"Do I even need to ask where you have been or are you just going to lift your skirt, take off your panties and let me watch you drip on the floor?"

His tone was just nasty enough to piss me off so I just stared at him for several moments and then I turned my back on him and went to the phone. I dialed a number from memory and when the phone was answered I said:

"Hi Mark, this is Lorrie. It has been a long time lover, feel like getting lucky tonight?

"You do? Good. I'm horny as hell and I was counting on my husband to take care of me, but I guess he won't be available for a while."

"Sure."

"Why not meet me at the Landing Strip."

"As soon as you can get there. I'm leaving the house right now. Just look for me in the back by the pool tables. I'll be the one with her legs spread wide and her panties lying on the table. Hurry lover, I need it bad."

After I hung up I turned to face Chuck. "When I get home we can try it again. 'Hello baby, I missed you' would be nice and a hug and a kiss to go with it would be appreciated, but keep the attitude going and you can keep me on my back with my legs spread for a long, long time."

I picked up my purse and headed for the door and as my hand reached for the door knob Chuck said, "If you leave Loretta, don't bother coming back."

"That's your choice Chuck, not mine. You decide what is important to you and what isn't. Just remember who had the idea that started all this," and I walked out the door.

The End

Here is a preview of a story you may also enjoy:

The

WAITRESS

and the

RUNAWAY

HUSBAND

HOT ROMANCE EROTICA

JUST PLAIN BOB

At check-out time I debated staying another day, but decided against it. We could always stop early in the evening and it would give me time to recharge my batteries. We had lunch at Mom's and as we ate Joyce said:

"I guess I'm still a slut. I was pretty blatant last night when I undressed wasn't I?"

"Did I look like I seemed to mind?"

"You are a guy. Guys go after pussy. I offered and so you took it."

"I guess I did didn't I? But in truth I'm not sure that I could have spent too many more nights in a room with a beautiful and sexy looking woman without trying something. And to be fair about it you yourself said you were a healthy female who had gone without for a long time. I just glad you chose me to be the one to end your long dry spell. I need to warn you though. Now that I've had a taste I'm going to want more, but if you don't you need to let me know otherwise I'm liable to take things for granted."

"Do you really think that?"

"Think what?"

"That I'm beautiful and sexy?"

"Of course I do. Why do you doubt it? Haven't you looked in the mirror lately?"

"That's different. All I see is me, but I don't see myself as others see me."

"You can take my word for it; you are both beautiful and sexy."

She smiled and said, "I think I'll stick with you. You are good for my ego."

We were on the road by twelve forty-five and we weren't ten minutes into the drive when she slid over next to me and felt for my bulge with her hand. "Have to keep you interested" she said as she found my cock and rubbed it.

"Good God woman. Can't you at least let us get a couple of hours on the road? You keep that up and I'll be pulling into the first rest area we come to."

She giggled and said, "I guess maybe I can wait that long, but if we don't come up to one soon maybe we can cut off on a side road and find a place?"

We did hit a rest area an hour later and I did pull in and park well away from anyone else. It was intense! Probably the risk factor had something to do with it. Anyone could have walked by and seen what was going on on the front seat, but I didn't care and Joyce sure didn't either. When we pulled out of the rest area Joyce slid over next to me again and I pushed her away.

"Stay on your side and at least let me drive until six or seven tonight."

"Spoil sport" she said, but she did move back to her side. After a couple of miles she took a book out of her purse and began reading it. As I drove I kept looking over at Joyce and wondered at my good fortune. What were the odds of my finding a beautiful and sexy nympho willing to pull up stakes and take of with me after knowing me less than eight hours? With luck like that I needed to stock up on lottery tickets.

We stopped at seven, checked into a motel and Joyce was peeling off her clothes before the door was fully closed. I laughed and said:

"Can't you at least wait until we have had dinner?"

"Nope. Got to work up an appetite."

We never did get to eat that night. At least not dinner…

If you enjoyed this sample then look for **The Waitress and the Runaway Husband.**

Here is a preview of another story you may also enjoy:

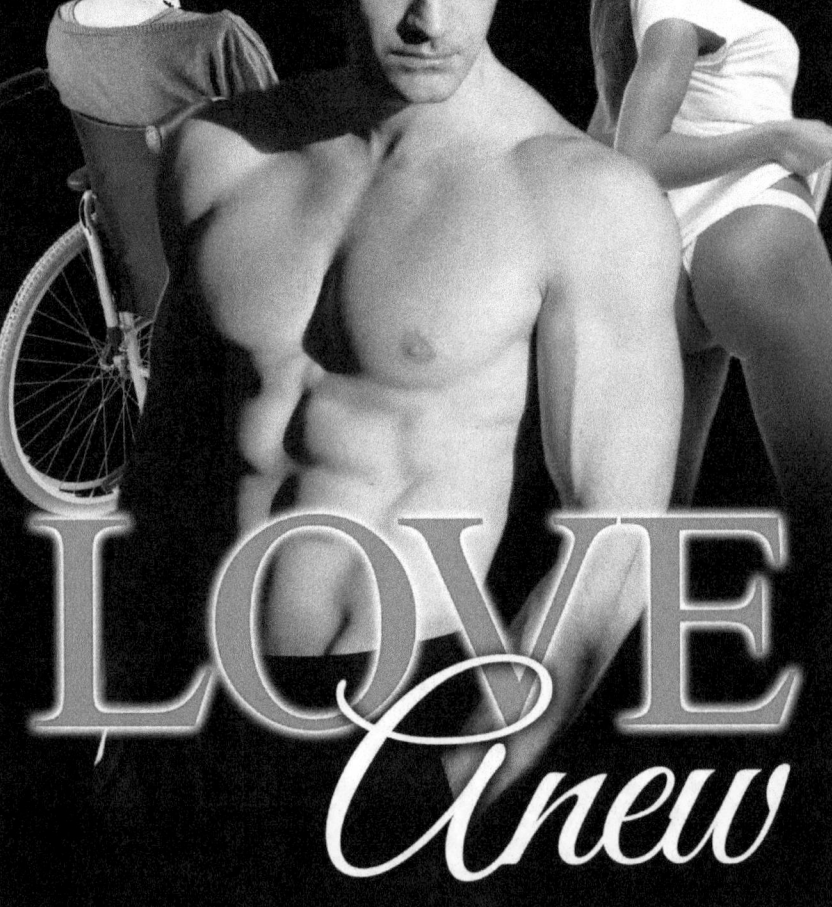

SHYLA STARR

LOVE
Anew

LONELY BILLIONAIRE ROMANCE SERIES, BOOK 1

Tricia sat in her childhood home and gazed at the wall. Today had been particularly trying. In addition to flying from Seattle to Dallas, she had immediately started to take care of her mother. Diagnosed with Alzheimer's, her mother also had a heart condition, and like always, had refused to take any medicine.

Before she had moved to Texas, her mother had lived in Alabama where she saw the effects of the Tuskegee Experiment that lasted long after the experiment had officially ended. African-American men who were diagnosed with syphilis in the 1930s were tracked for forty years to see the long-term effects of the disease. Even when a cure came out in the 1950s, the doctors had not cured the men. Instead, they told patients who wanted to be treated that they had already been given medicine. Hundreds and thousands of people from the families were infected and affected by the trial.

Due to this, Tricia's mother refused to listen to white doctors. The crotchety old woman refused to believe that medicine would help or that anything was wrong with her. After an hour of trying and failing to convince her mother to take the medicine, Tricia had finally given up. She had made some bread pudding with dinner and sprinkled crumbled tablets into her mother's portions. It may not have been the most honest solution, but it worked. Now, Tricia was just exhausted.

Moving back to the kitchen, she started to make herself a cup of chamomile tea. With her mother in bed, it was time to drink some tea and unwind. Thankfully, she only had another two days until the weekend. Her brother Tyrone had promised to take care of her mother over the weekend so that Tricia could take a break and catch up with some old friends.

Sipping her cup of tea, she went to the bathroom and turned on the bathwater. As bubbles and warm water filled the tub, she slowly began to remove her clothes. Only a few days ago, she had left John. After telling him of her decision to return home to her mother, she had not talked to him or seen him again. Their brief fling had been as passionate as it was short-lived. She had taken care of his wife during the final stages of ALS. Although they had tried to stop their sexual desires from taking over, John and Tricia had made love more than a couple of times.

It was wrong and she still felt guilty. Despite her ethical concerns, she found herself wishing that she was still with him. His confident nature and unwavering conscience had attracted her to him from the moment they met.

Easing herself into the water, Tricia laughed to herself. If only her mother knew that she had slept with a rich, white man. She would never forgive her. Tricia picked up Jane Eyre and tried to read, but even her favorite novel could not distract her mind. She wanted John more than anything. It was impossible for her to go without sex anymore.

After realizing how fulfilling and satisfying sex could be with him, she was not willing to go back to her normal celibate lifestyle. She glanced at the bathroom door and saw that it was locked. Moving her hand down her body, she closed her eyes and pretended that her hand was John's. Tricia ran her fingertips around the dark cocoa-colored skin around her nipples and then drew it down further.

Initially, she started playing with the soft lips around her clit. This was not enough to satisfy her for long. She moved her clit in slow circles as she imagined John entering her for the first time in the office. The sex had been so magnetic, so electrically charged. She imagined his hard muscles moving against her and moaned.

The moan startled her. She looked at the door to see if her mother had heard anything. There were no sounds from the rest of the house. Moving her hand down along her body again, she moved her fingers faster and faster. Tricia could feel herself approaching orgasm when a sudden sound surprised her.

The shrill ringing of the phone pierced the air. For a moment, Tricia thought about ignoring it and finishing herself off. With a belabored sigh, she stood up and grabbed a towel. It could be someone important for her mother.

Exiting the bathroom, she rushed to reach the phone before it stopped ringing. "Hello?" she said with a breathy voice…

To purchase this book, look for **Love Anew by Shyla Starr**.

Also by this Author:

<u>The Prodigal Family: The Abbotts</u>

<u>Watching My Shared Wife</u>

<u>The Waitress and the Runaway Husband</u>

<u>Baiting Mr. Little</u>

From the Author

If you enjoyed any of my books then please share the love and promote my books in Amazon.

If you write me a review and send me an email I will send you a free book, or many.
(Just know that these emails are filtered by my publisher.)

Good news is always welcome.

One Last Thing, For Kindle Readers...

When you turn the page, Kindle will give you the opportunity to rate this book and share your thoughts on Facebook and Twitter. If you enjoyed my writings, would you please take a few seconds to let your friends know about it? Because... when they enjoy they will be grateful to you and so will I.

Thank You!

An Open Letter from Just Plain Bob

A message for those who like my stories, those who hate my stories, those who are indifferent and those who have yet to make up their minds.

I have often stated that I really don't care what others think about my stories, that I write for my own enjoyment and then I offer to share. If you like my stories fine and if you don't, also fine since I have already satisfied my target audience - me!

It is human nature to strive to get better. If you take up bowling your first games are going low scoring, but you will work and practice to get better and as your average climbs you may forget the game where you had three gutter balls and shot an eighty-six, but that game is still there in your past.

Your first time on the golf course you shot an eighty on the front nine, but did you settle for that being your game or did you work to improve? You may eventually get a three handicap, but that nine hole eighty is still there as part of your past.

When you hired in at your job did you say, "Cool, I got it made" and do nothing more than what you barely had to do or did you go to work thinking that, "Someday I'm going to be running this place." You might never climb that high, but human nature says that you are going to at least try.

It is the same with authors who write stories and post them on sites like Literotica. Their first stories might not be all that good, but comments and feedback along with a desire to get better drive them toward putting out a better product or to at least try.

I'm no different. My first stories might not have been all that great, but they are still there on the hard drive. I like cheating wife stories and five years ago I found my first adult site that catered to cheating wife stories. It was a pay site, but it had a policy of giving a free lifetime membership to anyone who submitted five stories to the site. How hard can that be I said to myself as I sat down and fired up the word processor and went to work.

I sent my five stories in and sat back to enjoy my free membership and a funny thing happened. I started getting feedback, most of it positive, and I became hooked. I started cranking out more stories. The site I was sending my stories to had seven categories:

Bisexual
Cream Pie
Groups

I Watch
Gang Bang
Racial
SM/BD

I know nothing about bisexual or SM/BD and I had no interest in Groups so all the stories I wrote I tailored for the four remaining categories:

Cream Pie
I Watch
Gang Bang
Racial.

I turned out eight stories a month, two for each category, which means that after five years I have over 120 stories in each of those categories and they are all still on the hard drive.

A year ago I received an email asking me why I never posted stories on Literotica. The answer? I didn't know about Lit. I pulled it up, liked what I saw, and started sending in stories to it. All new stories? No, not hardly, not with over 400 stories sitting on the hard drive. Maybe one new story for each fifteen or so old ones. The newer ones are better, at least I think they are and I have received some feedback that leads me to believe that others think so too, and I will continue to write new ones.

But I am still going to recycle what is on the hard drive, stories that were written specifically to fit the four categories. That means that those of you who hate cream pie stories still have eighty or so to look forward to. Ditto for those who call me a racist; you will get another seventy or so interracial stories.

Those who hate wimps will only see about fifty more of those because the stories I sent to the I Watch category were split 50/50 between what some call wimps and some call "real men." Why the 50/50 split? It came from listening to the readers. I would get feedback asking me why all the men in my stories were hard asses. "In real life men are more forgiving, especially if it is the first indiscretion." So I would write stories with forgiving husbands and boyfriends and then the next batch of feedback would say, "Why are all your husbands spineless wimps" and I'd write stories that went back the other way.

Eventually I came to realize that I was wasting my time - there was no way I could write a story that would satisfy everybody and that is when I adopted my philosophy of writing for my own enjoyment and then offering to share.

As far as the gangbang stories? Well, what can I say? Gangbangs are gangbangs and there are still eighty or so of them to go.

The bottom line is that Literotica readers are going to see more of my old stories than my new ones. If I'm still around three or four years from now it will probably go the other way, more new than old.

I feel the need to respond to some of the comments and emails I have received. By far the largest percentage comes from people who say, "You are an asshole because all women are not whores and sluts and that's all you make them out to be."

Next most common is, "You must really hate women you sick fuck."

"You must be a wimp because all the men in your stories are wimps" is up there in the top ten along with, "Why don't you give it a rest and go crawl off in a hole somewhere."

There is a lot more, but I'm only going to address those four and in reverse order.

I won't stop and go crawl in a hole because I am enjoying the hell out of what I am doing and remember what I said, I am doing this for MY OWN ENJOYMENT and then I offer to share. Some obviously like my sharing with them and so I will continue to do so. No one is holding a gun to a reader's head and telling them they must click on a Just Plain Bob story or die. It is a conscious choice on the reader's part to move that mouse and click on that story.

When a man finds out he has a cheating wife or girlfriend there are only a limited number of ways he can handle it. If he loves her he can forgive, try to forget and try to hold on and somehow make things work. He can turn his back on her, walk away and get on with his life. The third option is to take revenge.

According to a good portion of those who send me feedback the first and second options are proof that the men are wimps. If the man takes the third option he is still considered a wimp if he doesn't do some sort of physical damage to the woman and her lover. These readers believe that the only way not to be a wimp is to kill, maim and destroy everything in sight. Doing that however, will invariably get the man throw in jail and that is why it so rarely happens in real life.

In real life most revenge takes place in the man's head when he says to himself, "I should have _____ (fill in the blank) the fucking cunt!" I know this because I have been there and done that (see The Dark Trilogy). In my stories I try to mirror real life so kill, maim and destroy are going to be for the most part absent. Outside of some fisticuffs there will be very little physical violence in my stories. Most of my husbands are going to do what I did, what several of my friends and others that I know have done, forgive, or walk away. If this makes them wimps and me a wimp for writing the story that way, so be it.

Next is the "I must hate all women." Nothing could be farther from the truth. I love women. I lust after women. I even like whores and sluts. I have been married four times, engaged two other times (that did not end in marriage) and I have always had girlfriends between marriages. My philosophy is that women were put on this earth for me to enjoy and I'm not talking just sexually. I could sit at the mall (and have) for hours and just girl watch.

The engagements, girlfriends and three of the four marriages bring me to the #1 anti JPB comment on the list.

"You are an asshole because all women aren't whores and sluts."

Well dear reader, you can not prove that by me! I will say up front that I KNOW all women aren't whores and sluts, BUT the majority of the women in my life were. My mother ran around on my father for years while he was driving a truck for a living. My Aunt Margaret cheated regularly on my Uncle Bill, as did my Aunt Mildred on my Uncle Paul. My Aunt Betty fucked around on my Uncle Bob for years and finally left him for his brother, my Uncle Wendell. Uncle Wendell in turn caught her on her knees at his company Christmas party giving Season's Greetings to his boss.

My sister is three times divorced and each divorce came about when the then current husband caught her out spreading pollen. Both of the engagements I mentioned ended when I found out that I was not the one and only and a lot of the girls I dated between marriages never made it to engagement status for the same reason.

And that brings me to my three ex-wives. The first one, Helen (I believe I commented on her in the intro to The Dark Trilogy) had seven different lovers before I found out what was going on. I was living proof that love is blind. Ditto with my second wife. She had a secret life that she hid from me and when I found out about her brother, his friends and the gangbangs she was history.

My third marriage ended in divorce because of a different kind of cheating (and I can just imagine the outrage I am going to get over this) - she cheated on me with an idea. I was away from home on business, she was lonely, a couple of Jehovah's Witnesses knocked on the door and my wife, with nothing better to do invited them in. When I came home from my trip I found out that she had found God. On a scale that runs from TRUE BELIEVER on one end to ATHEIST on the other you will find me just to the right of AGNOSTIC and since I would not allow myself to be SAVED the marriage eventually died.

So yes, I write about sluts and whores because as everyone knows, you tend to write about the things you know. And I do like sluts and whores, just not the ones that lie to me and cheat on me.

So be forewarned - if you click on a Just Plain Bob story you will be getting sluts, whores and husbands who do not kill, maim and destroy. There are other things you will rarely find in a Just Plain Bob story. Even though I try to mirror real life my stories all take place in StoryLand. In StoryLand STDs and unwanted pregnancies do not exist unless the author feels like they may add something to the story. Bad things do not happen in StoryLand unless the author so wills it and no amount of "You should have..." in comments and feedback will change a story already posted.

Lastly, I will touch on a truth. None of what I have written here means shit because the same readers will still read the same stories that they profess to hate and make the same comments they have always made. Knowing this, I will deliberately post stories that will have them frothing at the mouth.

It is the least I can do for an adoring public.

Thank you!

Just Plain Bob
justplainbob@awesomeauthors.org